Airship Daedalus

A Shield Against the Darkness

By Todd Downing

FIRST EDITION
ISBN: 978-0-9981989-4-1
Copyright © 2017 Todd Downing & Deep7 Press
All Rights Reserved Worldwide
Edited by Dan Heinrich
Cover art & design by Todd Downing

Based on the *Airship Daedalus / AEGIS Tales* setting and char-
acters by Todd Downing and published in various media by
Deep7 Press. *Airship Daedalus*™ and *AEGIS Tales*™ are trade-
marks of Deep7 Press.
WWW.AIRSHIPDAEDALUS.COM

Deep7 Press is a subsidiary of Despot Media, LLC
1214 Woods Rd SE Port Orchard, WA 98366 USA
WWW.DEEP7.COM

To the kid inside all of us,
who never stops searching for adventure.

- Foreword -

I ask the reader to bear in mind two things before proceeding.

Firstly, this novel is a prequel to E.J. Blaine's *Assassins of the Lost Kingdom*. Some might wonder why *Assassins* wasn't released after this volume, and the answer is simple. When I created the *Airship Daedalus* property (which has become known as the "AEGIS-verse"), I didn't think I'd actually be doing the long-form novel writing myself. My entire career has been spent in narrative and interactive design—and no small amount of screenwriting—so I assumed I would be producing the radio episodes, comics and tabletop game products, and hiring out the novels to other authors. Besides, the basic elements of this story already existed in the comics and radio episodes, so it wasn't clear that this book would even need to exist...until the muse said otherwise. Which actually brings me full circle, as I began my writing career in narrative fiction. With *Darkness*, I realized that because a novel can convey far more detail and nuance than a comic book or radio drama, it might be both fun and worthwhile. This presented an excellent opportunity to tackle a story I already knew intimately, and fill in some of the blanks at the same time.

Secondly, the events of this book do not take place in our historical timeline. The AEGISverse is predicated on an alternate history, with a few major differences. Aside from the existence of functional magic, lost worlds where dinosaurs roam, and practical weird science, the world powers presented (especially the United States) are a generally more benign version of themselves. Extended military enforcement of emancipation during the post-Civil War era led to the absence of a Jim Crow south, and earlier treaties with the indigenous peoples were actually adhered to by the US government, leading to fewer conflicts, more cultural assimilation, and greater mutual respect. I do not pretend the world is without prejudice or evil—this setting is very much a pulp homage and relies on dire conflict and high stakes. But I've removed some of the more toxic institutional ills, the historical persons presented are the best (or worst) versions of themselves, and the setting as presented is a more inclusive sandbox.

If you have already read *Assassins*, this book tells the story of how the *Daedalus* crew was assembled, and their first action-packed adventure together (and it contains a lot of material not in the original comics and radio episodes). If you haven't read *Assassins*, I highly recommend doing so when you're done with this volume. If you're a comic book reader, consider this book an issue #0.

Todd Downing

Summer 2017

- Chapter 1 -

New Jersey, April, 1925

Jack McGraw snapped his chewing gum and leaned left on the control stick, feeling the wind roll up under the belly of the plane as it banked into the clouds. His six-foot-four, well-muscled body barely fit in the cockpit of the Curtiss P-1 Hawk. Its frame rattled slightly with the sudden lift from an updraft, and Jack's stomach did a somersault as the air current let go and he suddenly dropped twenty feet. The plane was an Army surplus model from 1923, recently fitted with a brand new 500-horsepower V-1400 engine, which purred with each roll, skid and dive. Jack smiled under a pair of Resistal aviator goggles which hid piercing blue eyes. His square jaw—bristling with two days' beard—endlessly worked the Black Jack gum in his mouth. His boss, Jim Morton, had acquired a half dozen of these Army castoffs, which he hoped to turn into a working fleet for regional postal service. Jack hauled back on the stick and the Curtiss nosed high into the clouds above. He loved its quick response and control, even as the advancing storm winds manhandled its frame.

1925 was going to be a good year for Morton Aviation.

As he leveled out above a cushion of low clouds, Jack spied something in his periphery. Turning to glance down the line of his right shoulder, he saw another plane, then two.

Hello, he thought, banking into a turn to close the distance. *Two fighters in a reconnaissance formation? Not something you see over New Jersey these days.*

The giant engine revved, and Jack made up some distance, grabbing the pair of field glasses from their storage cubby in the cockpit and peering through them. He scanned for markings, for identifiers, even the basic body shape. They were Fokker planes, he was sure of it. War surplus D.VIIs, by the looks of them. Sleek biplane design, probably fitted with those BMW water-cooled engines from the latter part of the war. Painted pitch black with silver diamond wing markings... no... there was a decidedly concave sweep to the sides of the diamonds. Those were four-pointed stars.

Less than a decade ago, Jack McGraw had been a young and fearless fighter pilot, one of the countless Americans who had skirted their country's official neutrality to serve overseas in the Great War. He'd belonged to a squadron of American fliers in the Royal Flying Corps, one of only two aces from that unit. He knew German planes and German tactics, and this chance sighting set him on edge. He angled around to try to keep the sun at his back, but the black planes suddenly banked left and converged toward him at full throttle.

It was too late to hide—they'd seen him and were closing.

Jack leaned hard and flipped over into a dive, drawing the enemy fighters behind him. Four Spandau machine guns chattered in his wake, and Jack knew at that moment the pilots must be young and inexperienced. Battle-tested fighter pilots would always lead the target and fire in bursts to conserve ammunition. They certainly wouldn't have both followed in his dive like these pilots had.

As the checkered farmland of New Jersey zoomed up at him, Jack pulled back on the stick. He felt his stomach sink into his boots as the horizon dropped and the Curtiss roared into a steep climb. As before, the hostiles followed in the maneuver. Another staccato spray of lead and tracers flew wide.

Jack knew he was out-manned and out-gunned—his weapons numbering exactly zero. He also knew his Hawk had twice the climbing power as the D.VIIs, better speed and a slightly higher service ceiling. And he had the edge in experience.

But that didn't answer his questions: where had they come from, what was their purpose here, and what was he supposed to do about them—aside from simply avoiding being shot down? There weren't any D.VIIs at any of the airfields in the northeast region, of that he was certain. So they weren't local. If anything they looked like an elite offshoot of some Central Powers military force. But if that were the case, was the U.S. under attack by a foreign nation?

Jack leveled out of the climb at about 8,000 feet, cloaking the Curtiss above a bank of clouds, thinking frantically as the fighters pulled higher beneath him. Then the veil of mist beneath the Curtiss became instantly black and swelled up like the sea under a breaching whale. It surprised Jack, who throttled back and climbed again as a mammoth form erupted from the clouds. Eight hundred feet long and two hundred wide, the *Luftpanzer* was a leviathan. Torpedo-shaped and metallic black in color, the nose and tail fins were marked with the same four-pointed star icon. The roar of sixteen diesel engines cut through the air like its fuselage cut through the vapor. Jack couldn't remember seeing a zeppelin of such scale during the war, on any side. It rose through the sky in a wide turn east.

He felt his stomach leap into his throat, and his mouth went suddenly dry. In most people, such an encounter would have inspired a primal fear response. For Jack Mc-Graw, it was excitement. Who did this airborne behemoth belong to? And why was it here?

# # #

The bridge of the *Luftpanzer* was broad and cold, a latticework of aluminum struts and tempered glass windows, spartan save for the twin steering wheels and one duty station to each side. To port sat the comm station, an

Austrian radioman dutifully searching the airwaves with headset covering his ears. To starboard, the navigator's station, where a scarfaced, bespectacled Romanian poured over charts and maps of the Atlantic coastline.

Behind the two uniformed helmsmen stood the impressive Captain Jonas Ecke, sapphire eyes peering out from beneath the brim of his cap, a well-trimmed but voluminous white beard hiding a troubled expression. Next to him, a tall, slender woman paced the floor. She wore a black uniform almost identical to Ecke's, with the same collar tabs bearing a silver four-pointed star. Her officer's cap was pulled down just above almost-feline gray-blue eyes, her severe features accentuated by a short bob of raven-black hair. Shiny black knee-boots and jodhpurs completed the look. Maria Blutig scowled, visibly unhappy with the results of the day's reconnaissance.

Suddenly the radioman turned in his seat, one hand on his headset. "Alarm! Our fighters have engaged an American plane off the port stern!"

Maria spun to face the man. "American plane?"

"*Ja.* Civilian aircraft."

Captain Ecke regarded his associate with a slight tinge of exasperation. "Of course, Maria. We are in their airspace. It is not safe for us here."

"The American plane has seen us and must be destroyed!" Maria insisted.

Ecke glared with an arched eyebrow. "And what will happen when the local authorities discover the wreckage? When the U.S. government finds out?"

Maria locked eyes with the veteran airship commander and he could almost see the heat radiating from her gaze, but he didn't back down.

"Firing on this pilot is an act of war, and not part of our mission here," he maintained.

There was an awkward pause as the cogs turned in Maria Blutig's mind. The respect she maintained for Ecke, and the fear inspired by their mutual master, prohibited further debate. "Very well," she sighed. She turned away from the captain and barked at the crew. "Call back the escorts!"

# # #

Jack watched from a distance as the German planes banked away and took up docking positions under the giant ship. Had they overstepped their mission parameters by engaging with him? What wasn't he supposed to have seen? Something told him they shouldn't have been this far inland, and that they hadn't prepared for encountering local aircraft—a sign of poor planning in Jack's mind. He knew that in their place, if he wanted his presence to remain secret and he'd already fired on a civilian plane, he'd probably hightail it out of there as quickly as possible. It seemed like that was exactly what they were doing.

He glanced down at his fuel gauge and realized he'd been aloft far longer than he'd thought, what with the short but one-sided dogfight. There would be no further interaction with this *Luftpanzer* or its fighter escorts today. He'd file a report when he got back to the airfield and let the authorities take it from there.

The massive zeppelin turned south and became a shrinking dark silhouette in the afternoon sky, and Jack McGraw banked the Curtiss toward the patchwork of fields and farmlands below.

# # #

He descended over the new airfield at Kenilworth, dropping to a smooth landing in the dusty gravel. Turning the Curtiss off the landing strip, he taxied toward the midfield hangar, where a crew of mechanics would double-check the engine before putting her away for the night.

As he brought the plane to a stop near the hangar, he noticed a black Ford Model T touring car parked by the office. A couple of burly men in trench coats and fedoras stood nearby as a woman in a wool jacket and cloche hat approached the runway.

Powering the engine off, Jack hopped out of the pilot's seat and slid down to find purchase on the lower wing. He raised the flight goggles to his forehead and squinted as he watched the woman come closer.

"Well well well," said a warm voice. "Look what fell from the sky."

A rush of memories flooded back to him and he recognized someone he'd known years ago. Someone he'd shared a war with. Someone he'd loved.

"What the—?" Jack stammered. "If it isn't nurse Dorothy Brown!"

He smiled in spite of himself, feeling bewildered and attracted simultaneously. She hadn't changed in the six years since the war. Sure, they both had acquired some "experience lines" around the eyes, but she was still the same slender brunette, with the same mischievous, disarming smile and sparkling emerald eyes that made his chest hurt. The same feeling he'd had when she'd broken off their romance in Paris in 1918.

"Starr, actually," she corrected him, still smiling. "And it's been six years since I was stitching up doughboys at the front, Captain McGraw. I'm all grown up, with an M.D. now."

Jack reached up with a gloved hand and

nudged the flight cap back on his head, releasing a sweaty lock of dishwater blond hair from underneath. "Fair enough, Doctor Starr," he said. " And what brings you to this airfield in Nowhere, New Jersey?"

For a moment, Jack thought he sensed nervousness, but then it was gone, and the woman returned to her heartbreaking smile.

"I have a proposition for you."

Jack couldn't believe what he was hearing. He put on his best poker face and decided to indulge in some sparring. "A proposition? Isn't that a bit forward, Doctor?"

Dorothy Starr was in no mood for the game. In an instant her smile was gone, replaced by a look that was all business. "Isn't that a bit presumptive, Captain?" she shot back. "The proposition isn't from me."

Jack folded his arms across his broad chest. His leather jacket creaked with the motion.

"Then who's it from?"

The playful smile returned to her face. "Let's just say you won't want to miss this opportunity. Glenmont Manor, 7 p.m. Should we send a car?"

"I can take a taxi," Jack replied.

"Good. Might want to wash up." She turned and began to walk back to the Ford.

Jack suddenly blinked in a realization.

"Wait a minute. Glenmont? Isn't that—?"

"Edison's home?" Dorothy finished. "Yes, it is."

She arrived at the car and one of the men opened the rear door in anticipation. She turned back to face Jack and warned, "Remember what I said about washing up."

Then she was in the car and so were the men in long coats, and the Ford pulled away onto Coolidge Drive, leaving Jack McGraw one very confused pilot.

- Chapter 2 -

The sun had set in layers of deep orange and purple which gradually gave way to a starlit sky. A black Checker cab negotiated the circular driveway in front of Glenmont, pulling to a stop under the cover of the second floor living room which thrust from the house to overlook the front lawn like the eye of a cyclops. The structure rested on brick pillars and created a covered approach which allowed for guests—or Edison himself—to come and go without regard to inclement weather.

Jack paid the hack and got out, facing the east entry of the formidable Queen Anne mansion with a slight sense of apprehension. He cleaned up well, having donned a tweed sport jacket, gray twill trousers and a white fedora. He'd also rid his jaw of the beard which had cultivated over the past few days.

The taxi pulled away, and Jack cleared the steps to the front door, knocking tentatively.

There was an ominous clunk from inside as the bolt was drawn back and the heavy door opened into a lavish reception area. A butler in black livery welcomed him inside. As Jack removed his hat and handed it to the butler, he heard another set of doors open, and a loud welcome from a white-haired man of almost-80 in a powder gray three-piece suit.

"Come in! Come in!"

Following him was Dorothy Starr, dressed in a black dinner gown, with an expression that told Jack she was seeing him in a completely different light.

Edison moved to shake Jack's hand firmly. "Captain McGraw! Delighted to meet you, sir."

Jack couldn't believe he was being personally greeted by the Wizard of Menlo Park.

"Likewise, Mr. Edison. Please, call me Jack."

Edison turned, indicating Dorothy. His voice was much louder than it need have been, but he was compensating for his hearing impairment. "You already know our charming Dr. Starr."

Dorothy nodded, a slight blush to her cheeks. "Captain."

Jack allowed himself a half-smile. "Doc..." he nodded, then returned to business. "Forgive my impatience, Mr. Edison, but Dorothy mentioned a proposition. What's this all about?"

Edison grew serious for a moment, then clapped him on the shoulder as if they were old friends. "Not to worry, Jack. All in due time. Won't you come with me?"

The old man led them around the corner through a beautiful dark wood archway into a well-appointed drawing room. Jack stooped just inside the arch and took the room in. He could picture Edison burning the midnight oil at his desk, coming up with the next great invention to send down to the boys in Research & Development. The windows in the room looked west, opposite of the east-facing entry. Jack could see the dark silhouettes of structures further out on the property.

"Doctor Starr tells me you knew each other in the war," said Edison as he walked around behind his desk. He seemed to be looking for something.

"That's right," Jack said. "I flew for the 32nd Squadron RAF before America joined in. Met Ms. Starr in a French field hospital. She patched me up once or twice."

Doc smiled delicately at the memory. "Once or twice," she repeated.

Edison continued shuffling through papers and notebooks on his desk, uninterested in the energy exchange between Jack and Doc. "And do you have experience with lighter-than-air vehicles as well as fixed-wing craft?"

Jack shoved his hands into his pockets. "I've definitely flown more kites than balloons, Mr. Edison, but I did log a lot of time in British airships scouting for U-boats. If it flies, I can probably pilot it."

Doc interjected, "And can we assume you've been logging flight time on a regular basis since the war?"

"Yes indeedy," Jack nodded. "Mail runs and test flights for some of the regional aviation companies, mostly." He thought for a moment, then squinted at Edison. "Say, does this have anything to do with that giant zeppelin I saw today?"

"Giant zeppelin?" Doc stammered.

Edison found what he was looking for—a small key with a handwritten tag tied to it. He looked at Jack and soured.

"Oh dear," he said. "It's worse than I thought."

Jack squirmed. "Mr. Edison, maybe you'd better tell me what this is about."

Edison and Doc exchanged a look. Doc nodded. Edison turned to face the tall pilot.

"Jack, what do you know about black magic?"

Jack caught himself. "Black magic? You mean like spells and hexes?"

Doc pursed her lips. "Among other things,

yes."

Edison put the key in his pocket and circled the desk, coming to lean against the front. "As you may know, spiritualism has been an interest of mine for some time. In my studies, I discovered that a corrupt wizard named Aleister Crowley had created a privately-funded hermetical order dedicated to mysticism, the Astrum Argentum, or Silver Star."

Jack's lips became a thin line. Had the old man actually said the words "corrupt wizard"? As in, "wizards are real, and this guy is a bad one"?

Doc went to the window and looked out over the property, bathed in the fading orange glow of the setting sun. "On the surface, they appear to be just another secret society. But there's more to them," she warned. "A lot more."

Jack leaned against the arch, unwilling to fully enter the space. "I'm all ears, Doc," he said.

Doc turned and began to pace the room. The topic was clearly troubling to her in a very personal way. "Crowley has been deported from at least three European countries. His rites are associated with necromancy and blood sacrifice... What Mr. Edison didn't know was that Crowley's true motive with the founding of this order was to seek out and acquire as many mystical artifacts and items of power from around the world as possible, to fuel his maniacal ambitions."

"But... to what end?" Jack mused.

Edison nodded toward the door leading out to the west part of the grounds. Jack and Doc followed him outside.

"Only Crowley knows the true answer to that question, Jack," said Edison. "But I think we can assume his motives are not entirely benign."

Doc sighed. "Mr. Edison understates what we know to be true. We've been watching this organization grow since the end of the war. They've killed innocent people, and attempted to open dimensional portals to summon eldritch demons for personal gain. I actually have a theory that Crowley was behind some of the event leading up to the Great War itself."

"Which has yet to be proved, my dear Doctor," Edison added, underscoring what Jack interpreted as a fundamental disagreement between the two.

Doc frowned, but didn't press that part of her case. "He has disaffected people from all over the world flocking to join his organization, which grows stronger every day."

Edison led them across a manicured gravel path which cut through the west lawn. Electric lanterns on park posts illuminated the

grounds every twenty feet or so. "We have re-
ports of Silver Star devotees infiltrating government departments in Britain, Germany,
and right here at home."

"Does the government know?" asked Jack.
"Why doesn't someone do something?"

They arrived at a research laboratory—a
nondescript brick building with frosted glass
windows.

Edison smiled as he pushed open the door
and Jack held it. "Oh someone is doing something, my boy."

They entered into the cavernous lab, popu-
lated by several studious looking men in white
smocks who were pouring over notes and
specification sheets. Edison led Jack and Doc
toward his private office.

"Some like-minded friends of mine have
joined me in a particular endeavor. The American Enterprise Group for International Security."

Jack visualized the initials in his mind.
"AEGIS, eh? Isn't that a type of mythological
armor?" He was suddenly glad he'd paid attention in his classical lit class at Stanford.

Doc regarded Jack, impressed. "Very good."

Edison continued, unlocking his desk
drawer with the key from his pocket, and
gathering up a couple of blueprints from beneath the rolltop. "Since the Silver Star has

moles at the highest levels of government and conducts their war in secret, we figured we needed to fight fire with fire. AEGIS is a private, philanthropic network, with growing resources. We operate in secret, around the world, and independently of any single government."

Jack watched him close the rolltop and lock the drawer, slipping the key back into his pocket.

"Gee, Mr. Edison, that sounds great. But what does it have to do with the *Luftpanzer*?"

Edison herded them back out the door to the exit at the far end of the lab. Work tables were cluttered with amazing inventions in various stages of functionality, overseen by the bespectacled scientists in white coats.

Doc explained as they walked. "If the Silver Star is in possession of an airship like the one you saw, it means they can get to the most remote corners of the globe, extract whatever artifact they're after or complete whatever ritual, and be gone before any national military can intercept them."

Then they were back outside, Edison leading them further down the illuminated gravel path as the crickets began to chirp their evening songs. "To put it plainly," he said, with some extra pep in his stride, "people like Crowley thrive on chaos. They have no other thought but personal power, and they will crush anyone who dares get in their way. But nations in chaos don't buy American steel, or timber, or food, or airplanes. Chaos isn't good for anyone's business, or health, or standard of living. Stability, order, and a healthy population is good for everyone. So we created this 'aegis'—this armor of sorts—to be a shield against the darkness and unspeakable horror Crowley represents."

As they walked, Jack saw the shape of what looked to be a massive barn rise in the distance. The moon had come out and hovered full in the sky above it. "Naturally," he nodded.

Edison continued. "And to be the embodiment of this shield against the darkness, is a conveyance that will allow a hand-picked team of dedicated individuals to preempt Crowley at his every turn. To dog his every step. And let no trespass go unpunished."

The barn was now directly ahead, blocking most of the night sky in Jack's field of view. A lone work lamp set high on the outer wall illuminated a simple entry door next to a pair of giant sliding panels which looked to be on a motorized track. Jack could hear the familiar sounds of workers in a shop.

Doc took Jack's arm as Edison led them up to the entry door.

"Distances that once took months will be traveled in days," she explained.

"I don't understand," said Jack.

Edison smiled. "You will, my boy."

The door opened and Edison led them into what was actually an aerodrome. It was open and cavernous, with various heavy tools, machinery and work stations around the perimeter. Sparks erupted from welding torches, and the heat from arc lights above made Jack begin to bead up with sweat.

"What... is... this?"

In the center of the building sat an airship. It wasn't long—perhaps only 250 feet, if that. The slightly flattened lozenge shape of the outer envelope made it look torpedo-like, and clearly aluminum fibers had been woven into the canvas, because it shone and reflected in the dim work light. An enormous turbofan engine nacelle sat at the end of a twenty-foot arm jutting out from either side of the lower gondola, and it appeared to Jack that the cockpit or bridge was set higher up, thrust out just under the nose. A painter attached to a safety cable worked to complete the red stripe on the outer edge of the tail fins, and a winged sword and shield emblem graced the upper vertical stabilizer. Black registration numbers were painted on her stern: AX2-1. And along her side, level with the bridge, a name: DAEDALUS II.

"Behold, Captain," Edison gestured at the vehicle. "Here is your shield."

Jack stared, slack-jawed at the thing. He'd never seen anything like it—never thought a dirigible could look that graceful, for that matter.

Doc grinned like a schoolgirl who'd orchestrated the best surprise party ever. "She's a brand-new airship, Jack. With an experimental drive system."

The pilot took a step toward the airship and stopped, unable to pry his eyes away. He had a million questions. But all that came out of his mouth was a stammered, "Holy cow! T-That's one heck of a bird, Mr. Edison!"

Doc bit her lower lip. She'd missed Jack in the six years they'd been apart. Missed his enthusiasm and boyish energy.

"You think you can fly her, Captain?" she asked playfully.

He didn't look away from the ship. "Boy howdy, I sure wanna try!"

Edison chuckled. "You'll get your chance soon enough."

Jack made one more visual pass along the aerodynamic envelope and suddenly recalled the ship's name.

"It says *Daedalus II*," he said. "Pardon me for asking, but what happened to *Daedalus I*?"

Edison wandered to a workbench nearby and unrolled one of the blueprints from under his arm.

"Well," he began, "that is a tale in itself, Captain." He squinted over specifications and measurements as he spoke, relaying the story as if he were spinning a tall tale in an Old West saloon. "A friend and associate of mine, Vincenzo DiMarco, an Italian scientist living in Venezuela, made a rather incredible discovery in 1917, having to do with perpetual motion. Using basic principles of magnetism and nearly frictionless gyroscopic movement, he was able to create a small engine capable of generating deceptively high voltage. DiMarco was also a talented aviator and first implemented his engine in a dirigible of his own design, the *Daedalus*. He was to license his airship design to my company for civilian use during the war, but the *Daedalus* wasn't complete until the end of 1919. Unfortunately, agents of the Astrum Argentum caught up with DiMarco in 1922, and shot him down. Because DiMarco had no access to American helium, he'd naturally used hydrogen for lift gas, which made the poor *Daedalus* more like the boy, Icarus, who burned by flying too close to the sun."

Jack frowned. Edison went back to poring over the unrolled blueprints on the desk.

"We can only hope Crowley's men found nothing of value amid the wreckage," Edison said. "One of our agents managed to retrieve DiMarco's schematics and smuggle them out of Venezuela before Crowley's soldiers could find his laboratory."

Doc's smile fell at the mention of the lost agent. "Lucky for us," she added.

Edison pointed at different areas on the blueprints. "We built a brand new airship from his designs. Of course I was able to improve on some systems... the alternator, electrical battery array, and the controls."

Doc looked across the giant aerodrome at the *Daedalus*. "And she uses helium for lift. Not hydrogen."

Jack managed to crack a smile. "Well, at least if we go down, we won't be on fire."

Suddenly an abrasive Bronx baritone echoed out of the darkness behind him. "You catch my bird on fire and I'll pound you!"

Jack turned, astonished. There stood a stocky man of forty with salt and pepper hair and walrus-like mustache. He wore grease-stained coveralls and a mechanic's cap with the bill turned up.

"Huh? Rivets?! Why, Carl Holloway, you old dog!"

The mechanic reached out an equally grease-stained hand and Jack shook it, forgetting he was wearing his Sunday best.

"Woof woof!" Rivets laughed. "One and the same!"

Jack couldn't keep the stupid grin off his face. He glanced at Doc and could see her beginning to smile too. He finally wrested his now-filthy hand from Rivets' grasp. "Gosh, it's good to see ya, Rivets!"

The corners of the big, bushy mustache came up at both ends, and Jack knew he was smiling underneath it. "You too, Cap," the mechanic said.

Jack was about to launch into the multitude of questions streaming through his head, when he stopped, listening to the sounds in the aerodrome. Someone was singing. It was a song he'd blocked out from his time in the war. A song he hated.

Raise a glass to Captain Stratosphere

His head in the clouds, He who knows no fear

With his goggles on and his chocks away

And his guns a-blazing, He will save the day

Jack blinked, and Rivets gestured behind the group with his thumb. "I brought an old pal along."

Jack watched as another face from his past emerged from the dark. The angular form of the dapper British officer was clad in dress khakis and a tie, his wavy black hair slicked back and well-groomed, much like the pencil mustache on his upper lip.

"Well, as I live and breathe..." said Jack.

The officer grinned. "Thanks to me, as I recall." His voice was a pleasing timbre laced with posh King's English.

The men shook hands and clapped shoulders.

"Edward Willis," muttered Jack in disbelief. "Duke!"

Willis cocked an eyebrow and took in the group. "Looks like a bloody reunion of Yanks in the RFC, eh wot?"

Jack noticed that Doc and Edison had both been watching to see what his reaction would be to these surprise appearances. "Duke was the best munitions man at the Western Front," he explained. "And Rivets was the best kite mechanic. I wouldn't be here now if it weren't for these guys."

"That's why we recruited them," Doc informed him. "They're going with us."

Jack straightened. "Us?!" he puzzled. "Now hold on, sister..."

Doc bristled, presuming a chauvinist tirade to follow.

"Not to worry, Captain." Edison insisted. "Dr. Starr is quite necessary to this venture. In addition to her medical expertise, she is also quite the expert on the occult."

Jack started to protest, but Rivets cut him off. "Cap, she was with us at the front, remember? She patched us all up at one time or another."

Rolling his eyes, Jack reassured the group. "It's not the Doc I'm worried about. She can handle the worst the world can throw at her. It's just that Duke here took some shrapnel to the head at Verdun, and wasn't able to fly without vertigo."

Doc closed her eyes and chuckled softly to herself. The more she got reacquainted with Jack McGraw, the more she liked him.

Duke waved away Jack's concern. "Don't worry about me, old boy. I'll be fine as long as you don't take her on any loops or barrel rolls. Besides, if the Silver Star is really as much a threat as we think, you'll need each one of us in your corner."

Edison looked up from the work table, regarding Jack carefully. "That is, if our good captain is decided," he said.

It was like something out of a Jules Verne novel, Jack thought. He mused aloud: "Let's see… fly a brand new airship with an experimental drive system all over the world with my war buddies, saving the world from unspeakable horror. Fame, fortune, glory and discovery…" Jack folded his arms over his chest and gazed at the sleek aircraft. "I'm in. When do we take her out, Mr. Edison?"

Edison suddenly realized there was a timetable attached to the project. "Ah, we're still finalizing some adjustments to the battery array. Why do you ask?"

"Just the matter of the *Luftpanzer* snooping around over New Jersey," Jack said. "The more I think about it, the more I think they may have been looking for your little operation here."

Edison's gaze retreated into thoughtful contemplation.

Rivets stepped up beside Jack to look at the *Daedalus*. "You know, Cap... there's nothing on that bird that I can't fiddle with while we're flyin'."

Duke nodded. "I concur, Mr. Edison. If you think time is of the essence, I'd certify the *Daedalus* sound as a pound."

In an instant, Jack McGraw became the leader of the group. "Then we should take off at first light," he said. "I'll get my gear at the airfield and be back in a couple hours. Rivets can give me the rundown then."

A familiar chemistry coursed through the group, a shared excitement over a dynamic shared in harder times. A unity born of shared crisis.

Jack gazed out at the *Daedalus*, like a teenage boy on a first date. Doc took his arm again.

"Come on, Captain," she offered. "We can take my car."

- Chapter 3 -

The drive back to Kenilworth airfield was tranquil and quiet. Doc's 1923 Model T runabout chattered along the gravel road, its headlamps probing the dark, Jack at the wheel. He'd driven trucks—and even the occasional staff car—while in the service, but since mustering out, he'd been content to hire a taxi for ground transportation. He was in a plane fully half of his waking hours anyway, living in a barracks at the airfield as part of his compensation from Morton Aviation.

He decided he liked the runabout. Sporty little thing.

Doc tried to fill the silence by running down the design specs of the *Daedalus*.

"...and Henry Ford personally built the primary outboard engines to DiMarco's specifications. Her skeleton is a lightweight duralumin frame, and the skin is a new vulcanized canvas-aluminum fiber weave, laminated with aluminum powder resin."

"She's quite a bird, Doc," Jack replied, intrigued more than ever as to how, and why, they'd been set in each other's path for a second time. "Say, if you don't mind me prying, where's Mister Starr? I take it that's behind the name change."

Doc looked down and sighed. This conversation had been in the works for six years. It could no longer be avoided. "Colonel Dirk Starr, the surgeon I was seeing in France…"

"Right! The surgeon… that's who you ended up tying the knot with?" What Jack had wanted to say was, "…that's who you broke my heart for?" but that would have been unfair. Jack was a young fighter pilot at the time, brash and full of life. It made him extremely attractive to a battlefield nurse needing the warm embrace of a comrade in the midst of the hell of war, and they'd enjoyed a spectacular weekend furlough in Paris in 1918. But those in his line of work didn't have a long life expectancy. Jack McGraw wasn't a good bet as a husband. At least, not back then. She'd tearfully ended their fling to go back to her post at the field hospital with her surgeon. They'd lost contact shortly thereafter.

"Yes," Doc answered. "We have a daughter. He died three years ago."

Jack was struck mute. They drove along in silence until he managed a contrite, "I'm so sorry…"

"Thanks," she said quietly. "He's actually the reason I'm working on the *Daedalus* project for AEGIS."

Jack searched for a delicate way to ask the multitude of questions circling his head. Finally, he settled on the biggest one. "I don't want to reopen old wounds, but can I ask what happened?"

# # #

Venezuela, September, 1922

Dirk Starr stepped off the train in Caracas amid a scurrying sea of people. He wore a buff colored cotton suit and Panama hat, and would have blended in perfectly if not for his tall stature and dark blond mustache—a direct contrast to ninety percent of the Venezuelan populace. Vincenzo DiMarco's schematics for the frictionless dynamo generator and the *Daedalus* airship were tucked safely in a leather valise under his arm.

He scanned the crowd for his contact, Ricardo "Buzz" Santos, a Brazilian seaplane pilot who operated out of the Caribbean region. The man who would get him back to the States.

As he negotiated his way through the crowds of businessmen and tourists toward the sunbaked outdoors, a shadowy figure leaned around from behind one of the many tile pillars on the platform, raising the slim, two-foot tube of a blowgun. There was a quiet '*huff*', and Dirk Starr felt the sting of a dart pierce the back of his neck.

His hand flew instinctively to the pain and pulled the dart away. He opened his hand and looked at it. Amazonian native construction, possibly Chocó. He was tempted to look around and confront his assailant, but he knew it had been a Silver Star agent, and confrontation would not do any good if some kind of paralytic had been administered. He wouldn't have long before the effects would be felt. He just wanted to find Buzz Santos and get the hell out of there.

The dart in his hand became blurry. He shoved it into his pocket to take back to Dorothy. With the dart, she'd be able to determine the source and type of poison, and derive some kind of antidote. Starr had every confidence in his wife's expertise—he just needed to get home.

Blurred vision became blindness as Dirk Starr staggered out of the train station into the oppressive tropical sunlight. He felt a wave of nausea and he stumbled, feeling strong hands on his shoulders as he regained his footing.

"Señor Starr!"

Starr blinked in the stark white light, unable to focus. "Buzz?"

"Si, Señor. What has happened?"

The man was a murky gray blob in an ocean of light. Starr couldn't focus. He felt his knees wobble and his left leg give way again. Buzz held him up.

"P-p-poisoned," mumbled Starr, now barely able to stay upright.

He could feel Buzz sling his left arm over the shorter man's shoulder, bracing him against further falling. Then there was a car door opening, and he felt himself falling into the back seat. He passed out as urgent phrases were traded in Spanish.

When he came to, his vision had stabilized a bit, and he saw a seaplane floating at the end of a pier. Now Buzz was on his right side, and a man he didn't know was on the left— possibly the cabbie. The end of the pier grew closer and Starr realized he was being dragged to the plane. His right hand grasped for the valise, and Buzz noticed Starr's agitation.

"Do not worry, Señor. I have the case. We are going to get you home."

"Home," Starr repeated, and blacked out again.

Dirk Starr regained consciousness one more time. Buzz had delivered him to field agent Joe Salyer in Miami, who got him and the leather valise on a fast plane back to New

Jersey. When he opened his eyes, he was in a hospital bed and Dorothy was leaning over him. She seemed to be in conversation with an older gentleman in the corner of the room. Mr. Edison? He tried to speak—if only to tell Dorothy one last time how much he loved her. How much he loved their daughter.

But his vision went black again and the voices died away, and all that was left was the pain as his organs and tissues slowly necrotized. Colonel Dirk Starr was a decorated Army surgeon who had saved the lives of hundreds of Allied soldiers. He was a talented field agent with the AEGIS organization who had snatched the plans for revolutionary technology from the claws of a diabolical enemy. It took him eight weeks to die, in an agony he could not express. And there was nothing Dorothy Starr could do to save him.

# # #

"When he died," Doc explained, "I vowed there would be a reckoning with Crowley and his order. I've been studying the Astrum Argentum for the past three years. Their organization, their tactics, their magic... it's a terrifying thought, what their intentions are. And the blood already on Crowley's hands."

Jack drove as the headlights illuminated the road ahead of them. He couldn't blame

Doc for the choice she'd made back in 1918, nor for the course it had put her on. And at least she was back in his life. He could be happy with that.

"Starr was an officer and a gentleman," Jack said. "I was always a little jealous that he'd won your affections, but he was a good man. If I can help you find justice, I will."

"Thanks, Jack," Doc smiled wistfully. "I knew you were the right guy to lead this endeavor."

"Well the more I learn about Crowley, the more I wanna deck him," Jack muttered through clenched teeth. Then he changed his tone toward the positive. "You mentioned a daughter?"

Doc nodded. "Ellen. She's six."

"Where's she?"

"My aunts are scholars. Musicians. Renaissance women. They live in San Diego. They take care of her and see to her education while I'm away. I'll go down there to visit when we're done with this mission."

"I like San Diego," Jack reminisced. "Spent a lot of time down there when I was a kid."

Doc looked as if she was about to speak. She shifted uncomfortably and gazed out the passenger window.

"What was that you were saying earlier, about Crowley being responsible for the war?"

Jack asked.

Doc pursed her lips. "I never said he was solely responsible, Jack. But I can place him within a hundred miles of several pivotal events and meetings leading up to the war. It's purely circumstantial evidence, and the AEGIS board won't entertain such folly..." She turned to meet Jack's eyes. "But I know I'm right."

He believed her. Jack McGraw didn't know about magic and dimensions and demon portals, but he'd seen enough blood sacrifice and inhuman evil to last several lifetimes.

Jack turned into the gravel lot adjacent to the airfield office. He decided to steer the conversation away from personal matters and back to business. "Say, how big a crew can the *Daedalus* carry?"

Doc blinked, snapping out of her reverie. "Six, with full provisions and gear. Why?"

"Because there's someone else we need."

Jack pulled to a stop outside the main entrance and cut the engine. He stepped out of the car, and Doc followed.

"My gear's in a locker, just inside," he said.

Doc's curiosity was piqued. "Who did you mean?"

"Huh?"

"You said we needed someone else. Who did you mean?"

Jack dug in his trouser pocket for his keys. A small ring of four keys and a pewter Curtiss logo chain fob came out with his hand. "Remember Charlie?"

As he unlocked the entry door, Doc searched her memories of the war. There was much she'd just as soon forget, but the Cherokee sharpshooter from North Carolina with the dry wit and preternatural accuracy wasn't someone she could easily forget.

"Charlie Dalton?" She asked. "Deadeye?"

"One and the same," said Jack. He pushed the door open with a click and held it open for Doc.

"How long has it been since you talked to him?"

"Since we ran afoul of those fascists in Italy." Jack closed the door behind them and led Doc past the front desk to a row of pilot lockers along the wall. "My locker's over here."

Doc pursed her lips in the dark office. "I meant to compliment you on the Curtiss, by the way. Nice bird."

"Oh, she's not mine," Jack corrected. "Belongs to Mr. James Morton of Morton Aviation." He fished one of the other three keys on the ring forward and opened the locker. Out came a heavy canvas duffel bag, followed by a pile of flight leathers, cap and goggles, Army surplus web belt, and two leather holsters—

full.

Doc raised an eyebrow. "Well that's some flight gear you have there, Captain," she quipped. "You often find a need for twin .45 automatics in your work as a test pilot?"

"More often than you might think," Jack replied, dead serious.

Just then Doc caught something in her peripheral vision. Looking up from the duffel bag, she could see that the door to the adjacent airplane hangar was open, and that a light was on in the office at the other end. Then something passed in front of the light, and Doc had a moment of rising panic.

"Hey, Jack," she said, nudging him as he packed his gear into the duffel. "Is that Mr. Morton's office back there?"

"Yes," Jack answered.

"He must be working late," said Doc.

Jack looked up at the single light source from the office window. "That's odd. Not like him to leave the office door open at night."

Then there was a *clunk* from the office, and Jack's suspicion cranked into overdrive. "Stay here," he told Doc. "I'll check it out." He shucked both .45s from their holsters and began to tiptoe away into the hangar, but Doc stopped him.

"Oh no you don't. I'm coming with you."

"Suit yourself," said Jack, handing her one

of the pistols. "But take one of these."

Doc felt the weigh of the nickel-plated Colt in her hand. "Now you're talking."

"Just stay behind me," Jack instructed. "And don't be afraid to make a dash for the car."

Together they silently moved into the hangar and found cover behind a stack of wooden shipping crates.

"I can see movement in the office," Jack said.

"Who do you think it is?"

Suddenly a flashlight beam caught Doc's face. She ducked away, but it was too late.

"Hey!" a voice called out, followed by two pistol shots in the dark.

Jack grimaced. "Someone who doesn't want to be found." He squinted through the dark, remembering where the big oil drums were. If he could sneak around to their flank...

"If you could sneak around to those oil barrels," Doc suggested.

"Way ahead of you, Doc." Jack said. "I'll move around and see if I can flank them. You stay right here and cover me."

Then he was gone, and Doc pulled back the hammer on the pistol.

"I don't know if trouble came with me or you," she said under her breath. "But we're both in it now."

Jack scurried behind the stack of oil barrels mid-hangar. He poked his head over one of the bottom ones to see what he could of the office. A lone overhead lamp illuminated an office in disarray, with file drawers pulled out and furniture in pieces. Whoever this was had seriously tossed the office to find what they were looking for. Two silhouettes took cover in the doorway and traded gunfire with Doc. He decided to take advantage of their focus on Doc and silently crab-walked to the tail of his Curtiss.

He rolled under the tail, then ran—head down as though blocking for his college football running back. Before he knew it, he'd closed the gap.

"We've been found out!" a gruff voice yelled. "Get back to headquarters!"

Then a tall, athletic figure loomed up in the doorway. "Not so fast, boys!"

Jack was lightning quick, delivering two blows with the butt of his Colt. The pistol-whipped thugs rolled out of the doorway onto the hangar floor. Pocketing the pistol, Jack found the hangar light switches on the outside wall of the office and flipped them on.

Doc hurried toward him. "Jack," she cried, "are you all right?"

"Just fine, Doc," Jack replied, rolling one of the thugs over with his foot so that the man's face was visible. "Laid both of these jokers out for the count, though."

Both men were of European extraction, one large and stocky and one a bit smaller and bespectacled. Jack had noted the one who'd spoken had a thick New Jersey accent. They were both dressed in black overcoats and their hats —both Homburgs—had fallen away into the office.

Doc pointed out a gleam from the large man's coat lapel. A small lacquered pin displayed a silver four-pointed star on a black square field. "Look at that lapel pin, Jack," she said.

Jack nodded, deep in thought. "Just like the *Luftpanzer*."

"These two are Silver Star," Doc asserted.

"But what could they want with Morton?" Jack wondered.

Doc knelt and patted down the smaller fellow's jacket. She produced a sheaf of file folders and began looking through them while Jack poked around inside the office.

James Morton lay crumpled in a heap under his overturned office chair. His throat had been slit.

"Look at the files they took," Doc called. "Your employment records with the aviation company."

Jack reappeared at the doorway, face

ashen. Doc knew what that look meant. Morton was dead. She also knew why.

"They must have found out AEGIS was recruiting you," she offered softly.

Jack's mind was spinning. They should call the cops, he thought. With these two goons in custody it would be easy enough to bring in the Bureau of Investigation. Take some of the steam out of this international conspiracy. Then he heard a hissing sound, like the fizz from a Bromo-Seltzer, and he smelled something acidic and coppery. He looked down at the men on the floor.

"Say, what gives?!" he marveled.

Doc stood quickly, aghast. "They're dissolving!"

They watched as the thugs began to bubble and smoke, withering away to nothing more than a pile of bones and some empty clothes. Ghostly, vaporous tendrils of smoke drifted toward the ceiling. The larger man's skull cracked and caved in, pieces becoming fragments, crumbling away to dust.

Jack was astonished. "Holy... is it acid or something?"

Doc knelt again, her wits returning. "No. Look," she said. "They're decomposing from the inside."

"So you're saying this isn't better living through chemistry?" Jack asked.

"No," Doc said seriously. "This is arcane in nature. This is Crowley's doing."

Jack cleared his throat. "Shouldn't we should call the cops?" He didn't sound convinced. Finding Jim Morton's dead body had thrown him for a loop. He wasn't sure of anything anymore.

Doc tucked the files under her arm and walked Jack toward the entrance. "Someone in the organization will handle this. Let's get your gear and head back to Glenmont."

Jack started to offer a halfhearted protest, but Doc found his gaze.

"Right. Now."

- Chapter 4 -

Jack didn't sleep much that night. Between the murder of his employer, the mysterious disintegration of the killers, and the prospect of taking an experimental dirigible on her maiden voyage, his stomach was a jumbled mess. Edison had put them up at Glenmont, but despite the extra security and accommodations much more comfortable than he was used to, all Jack could manage were a couple of cat naps. It wasn't his first time feeling anxious about a flight, although the anxiety wasn't usually accompanied by such immediate peril—even during the war.

When Jack came down to the dining room, the sun was already peeking over the morning clouds in the east. Rivets—the sole occupant of the room—was seated at the table, passed out in his chair and snoring, untouched cup of coffee by his grimy hand. Jack was dressed for flight: khaki jodhpurs, black knee boots, and an open-collared cotton shirt. His leather jacket, gloves, and flight cap were in the canvas duffel bag he dropped next to the buffet table. He knew they had to travel light, but he also knew that they were going after some dangerous individuals, so he easily justified an extra box of .45 cartridges at the cost of a second pair of shoes.

As Jack poured a cup of coffee from the silver pot on the buffet, Doc entered the room, yawning.

"Morning," said Jack, handing her his full cup without missing a beat. "Sleep okay?"

Doc smiled, sipping from the cup as Jack filled another. "Hardly a wink. The airfield last night..."

"Yeah," Jack nodded. "The sooner we're up and away, the better."

Doc pointed at the snoring mechanic. "Poor Rivets was up all night, working on the ship."

"That's why he's the best," Jack said. "Hopefully he can hit the rack while we're in transit."

"And what about you, Captain?" Doc squinted over the steam from the cup at her lips.

Jack smiled. "This ain't my first rodeo, ma'am." He raised his cup to Doc in a toast and patted the pack of gum in his shirt pocket. "A strong cuppa joe, a stick of Black Jack, and I'm all set for first watch."

Another uniformed servant appeared at the dining room doorway with a platter of ham and egg sandwiches. "Pardon me, folks," the young man said in a reedy voice. "Mr. Edison says they're opening the hangar now."

A moment of electricity shot between Jack and Doc as they regarded each other in silence, then Jack grabbed a couple of sandwiches from the platter, downed his coffee in a single gulp, and turned to Rivets.

"Come on!" he hailed, causing Rivets to snap awake suddenly, snorting and spilling the coffee from his cup all over the table linen.

Doc tried not to giggle.

Jack gave a Douglas Fairbanks laugh and grabbed his duffel strap with his free hand.

"Goggles on! Chocks away! Huzzah!" he flourished, jamming one of the sandwiches in his mouth and headed for the west entrance.

# # #

The sun shone yellow and pink in the morning sky, reflected on the silvery surface of the *Daedalus*. If she was impressive in the dim light of the hangar, she was doubly so in the open air. Drawn forward by a tractor heavy enough that it wouldn't want to take off with the 290,000 cubic feet of helium trapped in the airship's twelve ballonets, she was a sleek chrome bullet, the AEGIS insignia heralding from the aft fin that Crowley and the Silver Star were on notice.

Jack strode up the gravel path to the hangar and his breath caught in his chest. The oversize thruster nacelles were shiny from still-drying paint, the window panes freshly washed. Every weld, every rivet and bolt and inch of canvas radiated light and promise. He was dumbstruck.

Doc tapped him on the shoulder. "Cold feet, Captain?" Her smile was radiant.

"Just the opposite," Jack said. "I can't wait to take her up."

The two strode the remaining distance to the ship, which the ground crew tied down to cleats which had been corkscrewed into the ground—angling away from the path. Doc disappeared inside the hangar. The tractor exited, and Rivets arrived, guzzling coffee from a Thermos canister, bypassing the cup altogether. He belched, wiping his wet mustache on his sleeve.

Edison was already up and about, pacing the gravel in front of the *Daedalus* while ground crew and mechanics made final inspections of their assigned stations. He held a fresh, unlit Havana cigar between his fingers, which he almost dropped when he saw Jack and Doc appear. "Ah! Good morning, Captain!"

Jack unslung his duffel bag and let it rest on the gravel path. "Morning, Mr. Edison." With hands on hips, he surveyed the full profile of the *Daedalus* in the morning light. "Well, boys, what do you say? Is she sky-worthy?"

Rivets screwed the cap back on the Thermos. "We had to re-mount the port thrust engine, but the pivot-head is working now."

Edison approached Jack with a worried, fatherly look. "Now, Captain," he said. "Remember to check in regularly along your route. Our network of radio operators can carry your signal back to our headquarters."

"Thanks, Mr. Edison," said Jack as he pulled his flight cap and goggles from the duffel bag and began to suit up. "We will. And you need to promise me that you will watch your back down here. The run-in we had with those two agents has made me a tad uneasy."

"Never fear, Captain," Edison replied. "I'm well-protected."

"What happened with the... situation... at the airfield?" Jack asked.

Edison waved the hand with the cigar dismissively. "Oh, you know how these gangsters get when they're shaking down people for protection money. Poor Mr. Morton refused to pay up. Then the gangsters were confronted by security guards, who inadvertently caught one of the oil barrels on fire, fatally burning the thugs beyond recognition."

Jack looked confused. "But Morton Aviation doesn't have security guards," he puzzled.

"It does now," Edison replied. "I need to protect my investment."

Jack laughed silently and shook his head. Edison was an investor in Morton Aviation. For how long, he wondered. It certainly seemed like he'd had his eye on recruiting Jack for some time.

Duke appeared from the hangar, draped in large-caliber ammunition belts and pulling a cart with some serious firepower in it. "What's our first destination, Captain?" he asked.

Jack shrugged into his jacket and closed up the duffel bag. "The *Luftpanzer* climbed and headed south, last I saw it," he said. "So south it is. Say, what's the ammo for?"

Duke smiled, his pencil mustache becoming a wide V above his lip. "Mr. Edison was kind enough to furnish us with a couple of Hotchkiss machine guns. 11 millimeter incendiary rounds."

Jack let out a whistle.

Rivets grinned. "They make a nice fire on impact, and the *Luftpanzer* is probably full o' hydrogen."

"Well then," Jack said, "welcome aboard, Mr. Hotchkiss."

"They'll be linked together at the top turret," Rivets explained.

Doc reemerged from the hangar with urgency in her stride. "Jack," she hailed, "the call just came in from Charlie. He'll meet us at Fairfield."

Edison raised an eyebrow. "Charlie? Who is that?"

"Charlie Dalton," Jack explained. "Goes by 'Deadeye'. We did some damage together back in France. I think he could be of great use to us."

Doc nodded. "I can vouch for Dalton, Mr. Edison. He's top notch."

A cool breeze ruffled the lapel of Edison's pinstriped suit. "Well," he mused. "It seems this endeavor is to be comprised of everyone Captain McGraw served with in France." He gave Jack a deferential look. "As it should be."

Jack sighed, gaze locked on the *Daedalus* bridge. "War makes for strange bedfellows, Mr. Edison."

Edison laughed aloud. "Ha ha! Noted!" he said, grinning. "Now we see the benefit of gathering a crew which has been forged in the crucible of life and death together."

Doc put on a leather flight cap of her own, tucking her deep mahogany curls underneath. "Bonds made in crisis rarely break," she offered.

Jack turned his attention to the group. "What say we take us a ride?"

Edison clapped him on the shoulder. "Yes, yes—away, my defenders of the good. You will have our support on the ground."

Jack shook his hand. "Thank you, Mr. Edison," he replied. "For the opportunity... it's a noble cause. I hope we're worthy of it."

Doc took Edison's hand and kissed him on the cheek. "Goodbye, Mr. Edison," she said softly. "We'll be in contact."

The group began toward the ship, and Edison whispered, "Godspeed."

Rivets and Duke went to the rear cargo ramp to unload the twin Hotchkiss guns. Jack and Doc climbed the folding steps in the center of the gondola, entering into the main saloon. The floor was a honeycomb of perforated aluminum deck plates, the interior similarly cold and mechanical. Some lightweight chairs and a table sat to one side, a small galley to the other. To the rear lay the crew quarters, engine room and cargo hold. The bridge lay forward, past the head with a single toilet and sink, stepping up to a ramped locker area, then a ladder up to the main envelope gantry, and topside facilities.

No wasted space, Jack thought. *DiMarco was a practical aviator as well as a scientist, for sure.*

Through another hatchway was what Jack had been looking for. The bridge contained a comms station on the port side, a navigator station to starboard, and center forward, past the emergency hatch in the floor, the pilot's chair.

Jack shoved his duffel bag into the locker and ducked into the bridge, heading straight for the helm. The chair was an aluminum skeleton with ample padding and leather upholstery. The right arm terminated in a dual-axis joystick, the left in a throttle lever. Foot-operated rudder controls sat on a low-slung footrest protruding from the chair. Rising on a thin metal lattice from between the foot pedals was an instrumentation panel with gauges for airspeed, altitude, attitude, incline, heading, and vertical speed, along with a gas meter for each ballonet and meters for each engine thrust pod. A red indicator said power was on standby.

He climbed into the chair and felt it welcome him. Taking a deep breath and closing his eyes, Jack felt the controls at his hands and feet.

Doc entered the bridge behind him. Her primary duty station was at navigation. "How does she feel?" she asked.

"Like nothing I've ever flown before," Jack said, and he meant it. Usually dirigible controls were large, bulky ship's wheels and winches. These were state-of-the-art fighter plane controls.

Duke entered and took his seat at comms. "All crew are aboard, Captain," he announced.

This was it.

Jack grabbed the radio headset from the hook on the left arm of the chair and put it on. He flicked it on. "Rivets, you back there, pal?"

"Affirmative, Cap," came the reply.

"Power on all electrical systems," Jack ordered. "Ground crew, secure all exits for take-off."

The workers near the hangar sprang into action. Jack could hear shouting from the men outside as hatches were closed and sealed, and the cargo ramp was shut. Bridge lights came on. Control panel gauges blinked to life.

"You've got full power, Cap," Rivets announced.

Doc strapped in, and so did Duke. Jack secured his harness and pulled the pack of Black Jack gum from his pocket, fishing out a piece and folding it into his mouth. Having picked up the gum habit in France to help with often-rapid shifts in air pressure, Jack now associated the taste of licorice with flying.

"Starting main engines," he reported. He flipped the four small switches for the forward thrust engines, then the two larger ones. The bridge hummed from the turbofans spinning to life.

"Engines good, Cap," Rivets said.

"All right," said Jack, ready to face the moment of truth. "Ground crew, cast off."

Outside, men released six cables through the tie-down cleats. The *Daedalus* began to rise into the air.

Jack leaned the stick in a slow, graceful right turn. He nudged the throttle forward. Engines whirred, the giant thrusters swiveled on their arms, and the *Daedalus* climbed into the morning sky.

"Course is south to Kitty Hawk," Jack announced.

"Affirmative," Doc answered. "Course plotted."

"Then let's get going," Jack said. "We've got some sky to cover."

The ground crew cheered and waved their caps as *Daedalus* rose to 2,500 feet, found her southerly heading, and disappeared behind a drifting mass of clouds.

- Chapter 5 -

In the chart room on the *Luftpanzer*, Captain Ecke was finding out firsthand how far Maria Blutig would be pushed before exploding. As a former senior officer in the German Army, he was used to being able to offer questions and even occasional criticism of battle plans and strategy when it meant lives at stake. The Astrum Argentum was clearly not that kind of organization. Maria ran her missions by a code of conduct stricter than any male officer Ecke had dealt with in the military. He knew her surname was an over-the-top affectation to inspire fear and obedience—nobody's parents named them "Bloody Mary". But she was still an unknown quantity to Ecke and most of the *Luftpanzer* personnel. He might have crossed a line. She was livid. Junior flight officers ran from the room or cowered in the nearest dark corner, trying as best they could to be invisible.

Ecke was no stranger to the tirade of a superior officer, but his refusal to back down only fueled Maria's rage. Someday, he told himself, it might just be his undoing.

"Do not lecture me, Captain Ecke! I am the commander of this expedition!" Maria scolded.

Ecke's breathing was calm and even, his tone soft. "I do not presume to lecture, *meine Führerin*. But surely you see the incursion through American airspace was folly. This is no criticism of you, but of Crowley's strategy overall."

"Did you not understand our orders, Captain?" she demanded, eyes wide. "We were trying to locate Edison's facility. Our intelligence stated that DiMarco's plans for his engine *and* his airship made it to Edison after our agents lost Colonel Starr in Brazil. That means while we were sifting through the *Daedalus* wreckage in the Amazon, Edison was building a new airship!"

"Understood, *meine Führerin*," sighed Ecke. "But we had far greater results with agents on the ground. Were it not for the interruption which called their essence back to Crowley, they would have led us to Edison's hangar."

Maria took a breath and softened, relaxing her posture. She knew that Ecke was not her enemy. But she was also in an impossible position, as Crowley's eyes and ears in the field. "Apologies, Captain," she said. "Crowley was adamant regarding the recovery of DiMarco's plans since they went missing three years ago. But the point is now moot."

Ecke raised an eyebrow. "We have new orders?"

Maria's eyes narrowed to feline slits. "Yes, Captain," she said. "Set a course for Pointe Quest, Haiti. Crowley has assigned us to locate an object of power there. And stand by for potential diversion."

Ecke snapped his boot heels together. "*Jawohl,*" he acknowledged, bowing at the waist. He exited the chart room with a long stride, happy to be out of her sphere of influence for a time.

# # #

The *Deadalus* appeared in the cloud-strewn skies above a makeshift airfield just off Lake Mattamuskeet, North Carolina. It was early afternoon, and the compact airship caused a stir among ground personnel and radio operators. The facility itself wasn't much more than a landing strip, a small hangar, and a private home which was also the terminal, airfield office and radio tower. Jack reasoned they could have found an easier rendezvous than this relative backwater, but keeping a low profile was higher on his list of priorities at the moment.

This was also Charlie Dalton's back yard. He'd grown up among the established Cherokee Nation of the Carolinas, some of the earlier indigenous peoples to assimilate into the dominant culture. The raven-haired man peered skyward and leaned against a US Army transport truck near the runway. Dalton had olive skin and discerning brown eyes. He wore Army khakis, with puttees on his lower legs and the blue shield patch of the 120th Infantry Regiment above the sergeant stripes on his arm. But the simple "infantry" designation didn't tell the whole story. Code talker. Sniper. Thrice-decorated hero of battles in Ypres-Lys and Flanders. When he saw the *Daedalus*, he flicked his toothpick into the grass and ambled into the house as ground personnel scrambled to meet the ship.

Jack McGraw angled the nose of the ship toward the ground. "Coming in over Fairfield," he announced. "What's the word on the wireless, Duke?"

The Englishman turned toward him, scribbling notes in pencil as he interpreted the beeps from the wireless on the ground. "Sounds like we're expected, Captain. Ground crew is standing by." Then another message came through and he grinned under his pencil mustache. "Charlie Dalton is requesting permission to come aboard."

Jack smiled. "Granted!" he exclaimed as the ship lowered toward the ground and the ground crew staked off the lines Rivets released to them. Doc tried to contain her excitement, poorly.

"It'll be good to see him again," she said.

Jack thumbed the *TALK* button on his radio headset. "Cutting the engines, Rivets," he said. "I'm going ashore."

He powered down the turbofans and let the ship be lowered and secured to the airstrip, as he shrugged out of his seat harness and headed for the side door in the main saloon.

Dropping to the dirt of the airfield, Jack scanned the area for his old comrade. Doc hopped down from the gondola and joined Jack in the search.

"There he is," she pointed.

Deadeye descended from the house, striding the path to the airfield with purpose. He stopped about ten feet short of Jack and Doc and saluted.

"Sergeant Charlie Dalton, reporting for duty, Cap'n."

Jack saluted back, then closed to shake his hand. "Deadeye! Gee, it's good to see ya!"

Doc stifled a giggle. Every time Jack let out an exclamation, it seemed the utterance of a five-year-old boy at Christmas. Nobody did gosh-and-golly like Jack. In fact, she didn't think she ever heard him curse—not even in France during the war.

Deadeye grinned back. "Good to see you, Jack. You too, Doc."

Doc stepped in to hug him. "Seems like forever since I saw you last," she said.

"Bellicourt, September 30th, 1918," Deadeye winked at her. "You took two bullets and a bunch of shrapnel out of me."

"That's right," Doc remembered. "I said you shouldn't have been alive, and you said..."

"I said I'd boosted my iron intake, and it seemed to be working."

The three chuckled at the dark humor that had been a requirement during that terrible time.

"It's gonna be good to have you aboard," Jack said.

"Glad to be here," Deadeye nodded. He pointed a thumb at the Army truck parked by the airstrip. "And I brought you a little present."

As if on cue, Rivets appeared from the cargo ramp at the stern of the *Daedalus*, and Duke dropped to the ground behind Doc.

Deadeye made a show of smelling something rancid. "What? You didn't tell me these guys were coming along," he joked. "I'm having second thoughts now..."

Smiles and handshakes and bear hugs erupted, the past six years catching up in minutes. Then Deadeye led them to the truck, opening the back to reveal a wooden shipping crate. Jack and Duke helped wrestle the crate to the ground, and Deadeye pried the top off with a crowbar. Sitting snugly within the crate was a console with a large, round glass display, surrounded by several dials and switches.

"What's this?" Rivets asked.

"It's called a 'radio detector'," Deadeye said.

Duke pushed up the brim of his cap. "Not like a normal receiver, surely?"

Deadeye shook his head. He loved educating the proper Englishman. "Not at all, Duke," he said. "This baby sends out its own wave, which bounces back to us. We can use it to find moving ships at sea."

Jack inhaled sharply. "...or a zeppelin."

Rivets looked doubtful. "Well if you're gonna use it to chase zeppelins, you can't use it for too long a stretch. That thing is gonna put one heck of a drain on the electrical system."

Duke nodded. "Understood. I shall sip it like a fine, single-malt whiskey."

As Duke and Rivets carried off the crate to install the console on the *Daedalus*, Deadeye retrieved his gear from the truck: a canvas Army duffel bag, an M1903 Springfield rifle with a telescopic sight, and a Winchester Model 1894 carbine—which he slung over his shoulder.

Jack picked up Deadeye's duffel bag, and

Doc hefted the Springfield. They walked to the airship together.

"So where'd this little gift come from, Charlie?" Jack asked.

Deadeye cleared his throat. "It's courtesy of the US Army," he offered. "But maybe don't mention it to Edison."

Jack stopped, giving Deadeye a sidelong glance. "Why not?"

"Because it was made by a certain Mr. Tesla."

Doc winced. "That old feud?"

"I can't believe they'd still be at it," Jack muttered.

"I can't believe Edison would still remember Tesla ever worked for him," Doc added. "That was so long ago."

Deadeye shrugged as the others hefted his gear through the gondola door. "Telsa's been working on some new stuff for the military—they're taking good care of him, but with the bad blood between him and Edison, I figured we might wanna keep mum."

Doc shook her head. "If there's any trouble at all, I'll talk to Edison."

Jack sighed. "Agreed. Until then—"

Suddenly Deadeye was unslinging the Winchester. A hundred feet away, near the stern of the ship, an airfield worker in coveralls screamed, "Death to Captain Stratosphere!

Death to the *Daedalus* crew!" while brandishing a bundle of dynamite with a lit fuse. In a single motion, Deadeye cocked the lever on the Winchester and fired from the hip, severing the fuse.

"Not today," he said, keeping the carbine trained on the would-be saboteur as Jack closed the distance and pummeled him to the ground.

"Hold it right there, friend," Jack ordered as he grabbed the pale man by the collar of his coveralls. "Who sent you?"

The crewman regarded Jack almost drunkenly. "Agents of the Silver Star are everywhere, Captain Stratosphere..."

Jack shook the man savagely. "Where is the *Luftpanzer*?" he demanded. "Tell me, you rat!"

The saboteur's face began to swell and bubble, and an awful-smelling smoke began to rise from his skin. The same process which had claimed the two agents back in the hangar in New Jersey.

"My essence joins with his..." the man said, almost joyously. "I become one with The Beast..."

Then his body was reduced to bones and ash, and Jack found himself holding an empty pair of scorched coveralls.

Doc and Deadeye approached with obvious

concern.

"What the devil—?" Deadeye muttered. "He just... he just..."

"Melted away," Doc finished for him. "I'll fill you in later."

"Did you hear that?" Jack asked them. "What did he mean by 'The Beast'?"

Doc's brow furrowed. "Crowley," she said. "He often refers to himself as 'The Great Beast of Mankind'."

Deadeye frowned. This was far more serious—and scary—than he'd assumed it would be. He put his trust in things that were real, solid. "Ain't met a beast yet who was immune to bullets."

Jack was suddenly all command. "Have Rivets check the hull. We need to cast off right away."

Deadeye ran aft to the cargo ramp, and Jack offered his hand to Doc as she climbed into the side door in the gondola. They sprinted up to the bridge, surprising Duke, who was still installing the radio detector console into the comm station.

"Sir?"

Jack grabbed his headset and strapped in. "Radio in to headquarters, Duke. Silver Star attempt on *Daedalus* ship and crew, foiled."

Duke stowed a small crescent wrench and slid into his chair, powering on the wireless.

"Affirmative!" he acknowledged.

Jack hit the *TALK* button on the internal comms. "Rivets, report. I don't want to power up engines if they're compromised." He turned to Doc at the nav station. "Shall we plot a course due south, Doc?"

Doc winked at him, but he had already turned away. "Aye aye, 'Captain Stratosphere'," she quipped.

Jack winced. He'd earned the nickname during the war for his strategy of pushing the service ceiling of his plane beyond factory specifications, diving on targets from a much higher altitude. He'd never actually made it to the stratosphere, but as a colorful call-sign, it had stuck. He wondered how the saboteur had known who he was.

Static erupted in Jack's ear, followed by Rivets' thick Bronx accent. "Hull looks fine, Cap. We're okay to take off."

Jack flipped each power switch in succession. "Get aboard, you two," he ordered. "Charlie, scurry topside and man the turret, in case we run into trouble."

The engine pods began to whir, pitching up to the whine of a swarm of bees. Rivets flagged a couple of ground crew personnel and told them to untie the stakes—or just knock them out of the ground. The *Daedalus* lifted into the air like an angry bird of prey.

In the pilot's seat, Jack throttled forward and nosed up, muttering to himself. "Crowley tried to draw first blood, but he missed the mark. And we're not sticking around to let him try again." He hit the *TALK* button. "Charlie," he addressed. "How's it look topside?"

Deadeye's monotone crackled into Jack's ear. "Looks clear, Captain!"

Jack made a southerly turn and throttled to cruising speed. "The Silver Star appears to have some reach," he offered.

Doc glanced up from her charts. "They do indeed."

"Which is why I want Duke to radio back and make sure all ground crews pass muster with AEGIS," Jack ordered. "We can't afford this happening again."

"Aye, Captain," Duke nodded.

"And Duke," Jack added. "Get ready on that radio detector."

# # #

The radioman on the Luftpanzer bridge clutched his right earphone and turned nervously. "Captain," he announced. "Our agent at Fairfield has failed!"

Ecke didn't wait for Maria to explode. Turning on his heel, he muttered, "Crowley has tipped his hand too early."

To his endless surprise, Maria remained collected. Her eyes narrowed. "Perhaps," she admitted, "but it flushed them out. And now we know we're ahead of them."

Ecke wondered what her game was. Any top-level strategy came from Crowley through Maria. Ecke was only responsible for commanding the *Luftpanzer* herself. Perhaps Ecke had criticized policy once too often. Whatever the case, he was not privy to the planning. "So..." he stammered, "we're not turning to engage?"

Maria pursed her lips. "Not yet," she said, so softly as to almost be a whisper. "As we fulfill our orders, we shall lead them far from their homeland, then strike when they are vulnerable."

Ecke turned to see her mutter a last curse, barely under her breath.

"Captain Stratosphere will die."

- Chapter 6 -

"Ready, Duke?" Jack throttled down and leveled out the angle of the airship's envelope. The *Daedalus* drifted forward on inertia alone, buffeted slightly by an easterly wind.

Duke signaled OK from his seat. "Ready, Captain."

Jack hit the *TALK* button and hailed the engine room. "Rivets, I'm cutting the engines for a few seconds."

"Affirmative," the Bronx mechanic responded.

Switches were flipped to *OFF* positions. Engines whined as they spun down.

"Engines off," said Jack. "Let 'er rip, Duke."

"Aye," Duke answered, flipping on the master power switch on the radio detector console.

There was suddenly a high-pitched *deet-deet-deet-deet* and Jack could picture the radio waves spreading outward from the ship like ripples from a stone dropped into a lake. Duke scanned the round monitor with discerning eyes.

"I'm picking up several readings," he said.

"Narrowing the band..."

"How about it, Duke?" Jack pressured impatiently.

Duke gently adjusted the band control dial. "Aha!" he shouted. "I think I have something!"

He sprang from his chair and turned to the nav station. "Doc," he said, "where's your chart for the Caribbean Sea?"

Doc stood and unrolled a chart from her cubby. "Right here," she said.

Duke poured over the map. "I picked up an aerial vehicle on a southerly heading. Estimate their speed at seventy-five miles per hour.."

Jack was back on the headset. "Rivets," he called. "How fast can *Daedalus* go?"

"Dunno Cap," Rivets crackled back. "There's no manual and we've never taken her out before."

Jack allowed himself a chuckle. "Good point," he said. "Then let's answer the question, shall we?" He pulled a stick of Black Jack from his pocket and jammed the licorice-flavored gum into his mouth. "Duke," he ordered, "shut down the receiver. Rivets, I'm putting full power on the engines. We've got a zeppelin to catch."

The *Daedalus* climbed and headed south until an Atlantic system threatened from the east. They adjusted course to follow the coastline to the southwest. Two and a half hours later, they were over Charleston, South Carolina. The sun was beginning dip in the sky, and Jack realized they'd be over open ocean during the night. This would be a real shakedown cruise, he thought.

After another hour, Rivets relieved him at the helm, while Deadeye manned the comm station.

The moon was just rising when a headwind found them. Jack sat, tilted back in one of the upholstered aluminum chairs in the main saloon. He gazed out at the stars, the soft blanket of clouds beneath them. Doc found him with his forehead pressed against the window. His feet were crossed atop the small square table. He looked exhausted.

"She's a good ship, Jack," said Doc, as if she could read his mind.

Jack didn't look up. His gaze was fixed on the waxing moon.

"Seems so," he said. "Quiet too—even with the engines at full." Jack could feel the envelope rumble.

"We hit a headwind," Doc informed him.

"I was wondering," said Jack. "What's our speed now?"

"We're averaging between 80 and 90 miles per hour," she said. "It'd be faster if not for the headwind."

Jack finally turned to look at Doc, standing over the table with a rolled chart in her hand. The years since the war hadn't been kind to her, yet she still maintained a natural beauty unmarred by the horrors she'd faced, the losses she'd suffered. Jack imagined her little girl —Ellen, was it?—looking like a miniature version of Doc, with the same dark brown hair and laughing green eyes. She was probably strong, and smart, like her mother. He wondered if he would ever have the opportunity to peek into that world. The world of a stable home and loving family.

"Like you said," Jack winked, "she's a good ship."

He sat up, removing his feet from the table and gesturing for her to take the chair opposite him.

Doc settled into the other chair, gazing for a moment through the same gondola window at the glowing moon. Then she unrolled the chart onto the table in front of him. "There's something I need to show you," she said.

Jack sat forward.

Doc traced a line along the Florida peninsula into the northeast Caribbean area. "We'll have to track them with the radio detector to be sure," she said, "but I think I know where the *Luftpanzer* is going."

Jack was intrigued. "Where?" he asked.

"If they continue their present course," she answered, "it puts them over the Bahamas, and then straight on to Haiti."

"And what's of interest in Haiti?"

"A lot, to a man like Crowley," Doc said. "Voodoo rituals, spells, fetishes, and very old Spanish or French religious icons." She pulled a piece of notepaper from her shirt pocket and unfolded it. "There are a number of lost artifacts of power in the area," she explained. "But his most-likely target is the Cross of Cadiz."

Jack raised an eyebrow. "What makes you think that? Just a hunch?"

"I've been studying Crowley's habits, strategies and operations for the past three years," she explained. "This artifact fits his modus operandi. Whether he's actually after it or not, it's something we need to keep from falling into the hands of the Silver Star."

"Fair enough," Jack nodded. "So how do we find it?"

Doc reached into her shirt, fishing a hidden pendant around to the front on its leather thong. "With this," she said.

Jack squinted at the shard of what looked like hematite. It was about $2\frac{1}{2}$ inches long and the thickness of a finger, silvery and rather ordinary looking, Jack decided.

"What's that?" he asked.

"It's a lodestone, of sorts," she explained. "Except it doesn't point north. It points toward items infused with mystical power. The more powerful the item, the stronger the glow and the pull."

"Wow," Jack marveled. "Where'd that come from?"

"Viking tomb in Ireland," Doc answered.

Jack sat back and folded his arms, smiling. "You're just full of surprises, aren't you?"

Doc flashed an adorable smile. "Did I mention I'm an occult expert in addition to being a qualified field surgeon?"

"You may have mentioned it," Jack smiled, but then the smile faded and his face became as earnest as his words. "But say, Doc, don't let that rock out of your sight. It's not something we want to fall into Crowley's hands."

Doc delicately let the lodestone fall against her chest. "I know, Jack. Don't worry." She looked into his tired eyes. "And now, as your *doctor*," she said, blatantly, "I recommend you go get some shut-eye."

# # #

Four hours became six because Deadeye fell asleep at the comms, and Rivets was enjoying the quiet too much to wake anyone.

Jack ducked onto the bridge, taking in the brilliant hues of pink and gold saturating the deep blue Caribbean sky.

Rivets heard him, and shrugged out of the pilot's harness. "Approaching Grand Bahama, Cap," he said.

Deadeye woke and made efficient work-like motions, which were lost on his captain.

"Great," Jack said. "I want to kill the engines again and take a signal reading."

Rivets just yawned and trudged aft toward his quarters. "You can do that on your own time, Cap'n. Far as I'm concerned, there's a bunk with my name on it."

Duke passed Rivets in the hatchway, and Deadeye stood to give the primary comms officer his seat.

Jack began flipping switches and adjusting dials. "You gonna catch a few winks, Deadeye?" he asked.

Charlie nodded. "In a bit, Cap," he said. "Gonna have a quick look topside." He ducked out the hatchway, climbed nimbly up the ladder and was gone.

Duke sat and picked up the headset. "Apologies, Captain," he said as Doc made her way onto the bridge. "It's been years since I was on a four."

He referred to the four-hour watch from his military days, and Jack nodded in understanding.

"It's okay, Duke," he answered. "We'll get the duty schedules sorted out."

Doc yawned as she sat at her duty station. "I really liked those extra two hours this morning."

Jack smiled, powering down the turbofans. "Cutting engines," he said. "Fire up the detector."

"Aye, sir." Duke powered up the radio detector console, which erupted in the same familiar *deet-deet-deet-deet* sound as the radio waves rippled outward from the *Daedalus*. Duke's eyes widened. "Well it's good Deadeye went up to the guns," he said. "Good God, look at them all..."

Jack peered through the forward windscreen. "What have you got, Duke?"

"A dozen or more small craft coming in fast!"

Jack hit the *TALK* button on his control panel. "Deadeye! Heads up!"

Charlie's steady voice crackled back in response. "Way ahead of you, Cap!" he said. "Seaplanes, look like Sopwith Babies—about a dozen. Pirate markings!"

Immediately, Jack was barking orders into the headset. "Shut off the detector! Engines to full power! Everyone hang on!"

The seaplanes buzzed out of the dawn sky

like big-footed hornets, spraying the air around the *Daedalus* with lead.

Deadeye leaned in the open turret atop of the airship, bringing the twin Hotchkiss guns to bear, but then the *Daedalus* banked and nosed down, and his shot disappeared—taking his equilibrium with it.

The planes broke and banked away, circling around for a second pass. Deadeye spun the turret to face the rear.

"Hang on!" Jack ordered. "Evasive maneuvers!" He throttled to full speed and hauled back on the stick, nose up in a tight corkscrew. The Sopwiths swarmed again, spraying bullets around the ship's envelope. Charlie could barely hang onto the gun grips as his stomach did cartwheels and he suddenly saw the crystal blue water of the Caribbean a thousand feet beneath him. Years of swimming and high-altitude exploration had taught him to equalize the pressure in his inner ear simply by swallowing, but even that was a difficult proposition right now.

Rivets half-climbed, half-fell through the bridge hatchway. "What the heck—??"

Doc gripped the navigation console with white knuckles. "Rivets!" she shouted. "Strap in or start praying!"

The *Daedalus* leveled off, having turned in a complete three-sixty to face the aerial pirates. They banked again, regrouping for a third pass. Jack squinted into the distance, and something caught his eye. A round object, hovering at the rear of the squadron. Then the seaplanes were all over them, machine guns rattling. This time, Jack gambled and took no evasion.

Once again, no damage.

"Wait a second," Jack said. "Three passes and they haven't hit a square inch of this bird."

Doc continued gripping the desk in front of her. "What are you thinking, Jack?" she asked.

"See that motorized balloon," he pointed out the forward window, "at three o'clock, south end of the squadron?"

Doc scanned the area Jack was pointing at. Rivets staggered forward, leaning on the pilot's seat. "The one with the twin Lewis guns on the gondola? Yeah, I see it."

Jack rubbed his jaw, deep in thought. "I'll bet the admiral of this pirate fleet is in that thing."

Duke suddenly turned in his seat. "We're being hailed, Captain!" He flipped a switch and static erupted over the bridge speaker.

"To the American airship, cut your engines and prepare to be boarded." The voice was a deep bass, with a Caribbean accent.

"Patch me through," Jack ordered, and Duke flipped another switch. "This is Captain Jack McGraw of the airship *Daedalus*. We mean you no harm and carry no cargo of value."

There was another burst of static and then silence. The four waited anxiously for an answer.

Static again. "Not Captain 'Stratosphere' Jack McGraw—??" the voice said, incredulous.

Doc cast a quick glance at Duke, then at Rivets. Duke watched Jack for a reaction. Rivets just stared at Jack.

"It's been a few years since France, *mon ami*," said the voice, and Jack finally exhaled.

"I don't believe it," Jack muttered. "Could it really be...?"

Rivets took a tone. "Care to fill us in?"

"Who is it, Jack?" Doc asked, leaning forward on the nav console.

Jack folded his arms and leaned back. "An old war buddy," he explained.

"Didn't you make any *enemies* during the war?" Rivets asked, raising an eyebrow.

"Plenty," Jack said, flipping switches. "Cutting engines," he announced over the radio. "Permission to come aboard, granted."

Jack unbuckled the pilot harness and gestured Rivets into the seat. "Rivets, you've got the stick. I'm going topside to receive our guest." Then he was out the hatch and up the ladder, and Doc, Rivets, and Duke stared at each other in silent confusion.

He twisted the hatch lock counter-clockwise and popped it open. The air was cool over the water, an occasional gust of tropical wind buffeting the small airship. Jack clipped one end of a steel safety cable to a metal ring on his belt, the other end to a thin guide rail which ran from the gun turret to the rear fins.

Deadeye saw him come up and raised his goggles. "What's up, Cap'n?"

"Stand down on the guns, Deadeye," Jack said. "We're receiving company."

"The good kind, or the bad kind?" Deadeye asked, climbing from the gun seat and locking his own safety line on the guide rail.

"I guess we'll see."

Jack kept a wary eye on the balloon as two diesel engines propelled it closer. It was a simple hot air envelope, lightbulb-shaped at the top, dangling an armored gondola beneath, on which was painted a name: *REVENGE*. The engines were mounted where propane burners would usually go, venting hot exhaust into the skirt, while two outboard propellers on the burner ring provided thrust. A pair of Army surplus Lewis machine guns provided an intimidation factor which was not to be dismissed. The balloon itself was a sun-faded

black, with a giant pirate flag sewn to the envelope exterior: a grinning skull over a single
horizontal bone at the center, with a dagger on
the left and a heart on the right. It had been
the historical standard of 18th century "gentleman pirate" Stede Bonnet.

A latching hook descended on the end of a
docking cable, and Jack pointed it out to
Charlie.

"Grab that line and hook it to the guide
rail."

Deadeye did as ordered, and a winch on
the balloon began to coil the slack cable,
pulling the gondola down close to the spine of
the *Daedalus*. A chain ladder unrolled, and a
figure descended from the balloon. Were it not
1925, the man could have just as easily been
stepping off a pirate sloop in the 1600s. He
was tall and broad, dark-skinned and dressed
in what could only be described as pirate re-
galia. A maroon sash and matching bandanna
stood out from the otherwise black ensemble
of baggy linen trousers, leather boots and arm
cuffs, and an extravagantly embroidered
leather vest which was cotton-lined and
stretched across a well-muscled chest.

The visitor turned from the ladder and
Jack saw one gold earring glint in the morning
light. The man's eyes moved from the Cherokee marksman to the airship commander in
brown flight leathers. A pronounced scar run-

ning from forehead to cheek across his left eye —yet somehow leaving the eye itself intact— marred otherwise handsome features. His mouth was a tight line, his jaw set forward.

Jack and Deadeye stood ready. They knew their position was tenuous, but they were resolved not to be taken prisoner or lose the *Daedalus* to sky pirates. If need be, they would die defending the ship—or see it destroyed.

"Well well well," boomed the pirate captain over the buffeting wind. "If it isn't the one and only Captain Stratosphere."

At over six feet tall, Jack was still outsized by the man. Even so, he stuck out his chest in a misplaced show of courage.

"Captain Stede Bonnet of the Lafayette Escadrille," Jack announced.

The pirate stepped forward, towering menacingly.

"I never got a chance to do this back in France," he said, his voice thrumming like distant cannon fire.

Then he grabbed Jack in a massive bear hug, lifting him into the air such that his safety cable clanked and pulled at the guide rail. He put Jack down, grasping both of his shoulders in massive hands. "Thank you for saving my life, my friend," he beamed.

Deadeye exhaled, and Jack allowed himself

a nervous chuckle.

"Good to see you, Stede," Jack said. "I wasn't sure what reception we were gonna get. It's been a few years since the war."

"Nonsense!" Bonnet laughed. "I would not forget the man who saved my skin! We must have some rum and celebrate old comrades-in-arms!"

Jack realized that they were outside United States jurisdiction, therefore Prohibition didn't apply. In reality, he'd rarely had to worry about it in the States anyway, since everyone seemed to have a way around it. He couldn't remember ever having tasted rum, but he was certainly willing to try it.

The pirate seaplanes turned and descended over Grand Bahama, and Captain Bonnet directed the *Daedalus* down to the harbor at West End, at the northwest tip of the island. Stede leaned on the pilot seat and marveled at the bridge as Jack gave him a general rundown of the airship's capabilities.

West End was a small tropical island community rising from the sea. White stucco houses and red tile roofs punctuated a strip of green palms and white sand, and busy locals bustled to and fro, engaged in trade or less-savory business. An oil tanker lay on the beach just east of the harbor, being dismantled for scrap. Pirate seaplanes and commercial boats crowded the tiny harbor, coming and going with cargo to sell or empty holds to fill.

They tied down at a pier usually reserved for large fishing boats or supply ships, and Stede informed his pirates that the *Daedalus* crew were to be treated as honored guests.

Then Jack and Doc joined him to go get drunk.

- Chapter 7 -

France, May, 1918

Stede Bonnet pushed forward on the stick, nosing his SPAD VII into a dive. He was separated from his squadron and miles beyond the German lines. He desperately needed to shake the enemy pilot on his six. But the forest green Fokker triplane matched the maneuver and let loose a volley of hot lead from a pair of synchronized Spandau machine guns.

A line of holes perforated the SPAD's fuselage. The last bullet shattered the small windscreen, and a sudden sting told Bonnet he'd been grazed as well.

He pulled back hard on the stick, kicking to full throttle as the SPAD climbed high into the clouds. Maybe he could hide away from this German flier, who seemed to be able to match his every move. He banked the biplane toward the Lafayette Escadrille aerodrome just outside Verdun, squinting through the clouds for a landmark below. Stede knew the green plane and black Iron Cross insignia belonged to German ace Hans Heinrich, and he felt sick, because Heinrich was a pilot known for enforcing kills in the air. Whereas many pilots considered themselves gentlemen and would only shoot to disable enemy planes, allowing the pilots to survive, Heinrich always went for a total kill.

Stede felt wet on his neck and reached up to wipe blood onto the fingers of his gloves. His goggles were cracked on the left side, probably from the piece of windscreen which had impacted his head as it was blown apart by the German machine guns. Blood ran from a wound on his forehead and cheek, above and below the broken goggles.

Lifting the goggles to his leather flight cap, Stede strained to see ahead, but the lack of windscreen and functional eye protection already had his vision murky with tears.

He dove, deciding it best to take his chances while still able to read the landmarks below. The Fokker was immediately behind him, spraying the SPAD with another line of bullet holes. The Hispano-Suiza V8 engine sputtered and revved, sputtered and revved, and Stede knew immediately that the fuel line had been hit. He hauled left and right on the stick, jinking and weaving as Heinrich closed for the kill.

Suddenly a blue S.E.5 with British wing markings came screaming out of the sun above Heinrich, opening up with the staccato harmony of a Vickers machine gun and a top-wing-mounted Lewis gun. The Fokker erupted in smoke and fire, Heinrich struggling to maintain control of his plane as flames leaped into the cockpit. Another burst of gunfire from the S.E.5 tore through Heinrich himself, ensuring he would not feel the fire nor the impact as his plane spiraled down in smoldering wreckage.

Stede glanced to his left. Blood was seeping into his left eye, but he could just make out the pilot of the British plane. A square-jawed six-footer saluted him and drifted back to fly escort until Stede got his failing plane close to home. Then the British plane was gone.

Stede Bonnet followed up with the other Allied squadrons, asking after the blue S.E.5 and its pilot. He'd managed to get a name: Jack McGraw, the pilot they called "Captain Stratosphere" for his tactics, which sounded quite like the pilot he'd encountered. Jack had likewise found the pale yellow SPAD with the black skull markings to belong to Lieutenant Stede Bonnet with the Escadrille Américaine. The two men had come close to meeting over the next few months, but then the RAF No. 32 Squadron was reassigned back to England after the Armistice, and McGraw with it. For two pilots who had only met briefly in the skies over France, each ended the war knowing quite a bit about the other.

# # #

The tavern was like a swashbuckler movie set. Stucco outside, exposed brick within, wrought-iron candle lanterns on the walls and hanging from the ceiling beams—strong enough to swing on, Jack thought. Fishermen and pilots mixed with the local prostitutes, and a one-eyed bartender pulled frothy beers from wooden casks behind the bar. Rum bottles—of a locally-made and unmarked variety—lined the shelves above.

Doc felt as if she'd wandered into a Robert Louis Stevenson novel.

Stede, Jack and Doc sat at a quiet corner table. The trio occasionally got a discerning look from one of the patrons, but nobody messed with Stede Bonnet, pirate admiral of the skies.

A small monkey scampered among the three, taking the occasional scrap of food or nip of rum from Stede's glass.

Stede was catching his guests up on his transition out of the French military.

"So when the war ended," he explained, "most of us found a distinct lack of opportunity out here in the islands. There weren't any jobs before the war, after all. I don't know what I thought would be different." He took a gulp from the glass, swallowing hard. "So we cobbled together this flying flotilla and made our own opportunity."

"What about running mail or passenger service?" Jack asked.

"We do that too," Stede nodded. "But the legal jobs are few, and they don't pay well."

The monkey suddenly climbed up on Doc's shoulder and began to groom her, combing through her hair for anything edible.

Stede laughed. "It would appear you've become the new best friend of Jake-in-Irons."

Doc grinned as the monkey dug into her hair. "What a jolly pirate name," she said.

"We took him from a South African poacher who sailed into our jurisdiction," Stede said. "It seemed appropriate." He tipped back another sip of rum. "But enough about me. What brings you to my island, Captain?"

Jack leaned forward on his elbows. "What else," he asked, "but the end of the world?"

They sat and talked for another hour, telling Stede the story of Aleister Crowley and the Silver Star, of the mysterious *Luftpanzer*, of the assassinations of Vincenzo DiMarco and Dirk Starr, and the origin of AEGIS and the airship *Daedalus*. When they were finished, Stede leaned back in the corner, tossing a shot of rum back and mulling over this new information.

He glanced back and forth at Jack and Doc, finally sitting forward. "That's quite a tale," he said.

"God's own truth, Stede." Jack ran a hand through his hair and noticed it was matted with sweat. The Caribbean was a region where you just accepted you were going to be wet at all times with seawater, rain, sweat, or a combination of all three.

Jake-in-Irons had passed out, belly full and distended, in Doc's lap. She spoke softly so as not to wake him.

"We think the *Luftpanzer* might be on its way to Haiti," she suggested. "Possibly to acquire the Cross of Cadiz."

Stede leaned back again, holding the small pewter mug with three fingers. "Doc," he said, "I might not go in for all of that occult mumbo jumbo, but the bottom line is that Jack here saved my life. So 'end of the world' or no, Bonnet's Brigands will give the *Daedalus* crew safe passage within our skies, and we'll help you whenever we can."

He offered the mug to Jack, who toasted with his own. "Thank you, dear friend."

Then the sky above West End became suddenly dark, and a behemoth descended from the clouds. The bar began to clear, and Deadeye burst into the tavern from the street outside.

"Captain!" he shouted. "Picked up a huge signal—Duke thinks it's the *Luftpanzer*!"

The plaintive wail of an emergency siren rose above the confusion of patrons scattering. Stede rose from the table and headed for the front entrance. "They must be close," he said.

Jack and Doc met Deadeye at the door.

"Take Doc back to the ship," Jack ordered. "I'll be there as fast as I can."

The first explosion tore through the bottle glass window of the tavern, knocking the four to the ground.

Stede was up immediately, rushing outside —and taking the door off its hinges in the process. Another explosion rocked the town center, then another, then another. The old cobblestone streets were strewn with ceramic roof tiles and chunks of plaster. Parts of at least six bodies poked up through the rubble.

"They're bombing us!" Stede bellowed, furious. He took off down the street, Jack following behind.

"Doc! Over here!" Deadeye grabbed Doc by the shoulder, hauling her toward the small electric motorcycle parked near the outside tavern door. The Dugdale had a lightweight aluminum frame and a bolt-on sidecar, which wasn't much more than a folding baby carriage with an armor plate at the front. Deadeye jumped into the saddle, switching on the underpowered electric engine. Doc stumbled into the sidecar, finding an uncomfortable seat on a honeycombed piece of metal.

The bike pulled away with a whine, just as another bomb impacted the street, sending chunks of dirt, cobblestones and 300-year-old tar into the air in front of them. Deadeye struggled to keep the motorcycle upright, almost spilling them both as the front fork caught a pothole and flipped sideways. He readjusted in the air and the bike came down hard, rubber tires squeaking on the cobbles.

Doc grunted with the impact. "Oof! I was never thrilled with the Dugdale," she said.

Deadeye revved the electric motor to full throttle, slaloming down the main street to the harbor, dodging bombs and debris. "It's light, it's fast, and it'll get us back to the ship," he said.

Two streets to the west, Jack caught up with Stede. The pirate was heading toward a pier that branched off from the main dock, where a couple of Sopwith Babies floated at the wharf.

"Got a spare kite you could let me fly?" Jack asked.

"Thought you'd never ask," Stede replied. "This way—to the north dock!"

The two men scampered over a low retaining wall and down across a spit of sand to the makeshift air harbor, where Stede jumped into the *Revenge* gondola, casting off the dock ties immediately.

Jack undid a dock line on a Sopwith Baby, climbed into the cockpit and hit the ignition. He thrilled as the Clerget rotary engine spun to life, and he shoved a piece of Black Jack gum into his mouth as he pulled away into the water of the harbor. He did a quick visual check of the flaps and rudder as he pulled the radio headset from its cubby and taxied into the bay to take off.

The *Revenge* had 600 feet of altitude on him before he was off the water.

Jack put on the Resistal goggles he'd brought along, grabbing the pinch-call on the radio. "Captain McGraw to *Daedalus*," he said. "Climb as high as you can. Get out of the area. Defend the ship if necessary, but do not engage. We'll handle the *Luftpanzer*!"

The frequency was already abuzz with pirate chatter, wondering what kind of ship could appear out of the clouds and bomb their town. Most of the pirate seaplanes had already scrambled aloft and were racing to engage the attacker.

Jack watched in horror as two Sopwiths were blown to pieces as they approached the giant airship, shredded by heavy machine gun fire from gun emplacements amidships. Then his fuselage was dotted with bullet holes and a

Fokker D.VII swooped past him. He throttled forward and climbed slightly to get some altitude on the Silver Star plane. "Come here, you dirty rat!"

Static burst into his ears, and Jack heard Stede's voice. "Watch your tail, Jack," he warned. "Two enemy fighters coming in fast!"

Jack ventured a quick look behind his plane to see two more Silver Star fighters drafting in on him. He banked to the left, but the Sopwith felt slower than he was used to—probably the floats. The enemy fighters easily tracked with him.

"Stede, I can't shake 'em!" He pulled back on the stick in a high corkscrew maneuver, his favorite evasive action. At 4,000 feet, he arched over backwards, feeling the few moments of weightlessness before gravity took hold and pulled him down with the plane. The *Revenge* motored almost half a mile directly below him. He used the balloon as a visual reference as the plane dove almost vertically. The Silver Star fighters stuck with him, diving in unison.

Stede was back in Jack's ears. "When you dive, bank right and roll under the *Revenge*. Bring them to my guns!"

Jack aimed for the edge of the *Revenge's* gondola, waiting until the last possible moment to bank sideways under the balloon, rolling as he did so. His left float brushed the gondola's undercarriage as it flipped over with the rolling Sopwith.

Stede's Lewis guns barked, and shredded one of the enemy planes' upper wings clean off. The plane spiraled to the water and splashed down.

"Great shot, Stede!" Jack shouted.

He leveled out and throttled back, and the other Silver Star plane shot past him, its pilot anticipating a wholly different position. Jack opened up with the Sopwith's Lewis gun and picked apart the enemy's tail rudder and link-ages. The fighter skidded sideways, presenting Jack with a larger target. He fired again, and the pilot was ripped into bloody pieces along with the flight controls. One of the Spandau guns popped loose and fell into the spinning propeller, sending pieces of both flying in every direction. The dead pilot immediately began to smoke and bubble, and the D.VII dropped toward the water like a falling anchor.

Jack throttled forward again and pulled back on the stick, aiming for the top side of the *Luftpanzer*. If he approached from dead astern, he figured he'd stand a better chance of not getting shot by those machine guns in the middle.

"Now to see what this zeppelin is made of," Jack broadcast. "All Brigands, form up on me and we'll take a run up its backside!" Then he added,"Use incendiaries if you have 'em!"

The pirate squadron gathered on Jack's wings and tail, eleven seaplanes and a powered balloon. The *Daedalus* brought up the rear at an altitude of 6,000 feet. Even at full speed, the *Luftpanzer* was no match for the Sopwiths, which could clock 100 miles per hour. It began to climb and run, and Jack prepared to strafe it.

"First wave, on me!" he shouted, pushing forward on the stick and throttling to full speed.

But as the pirate planes neared their target, the giant airship began to emit an unearthly glow, and a whistling feedback saturated their headsets. The glow became an ever brighter light, culminating in a blinding flash...

...then nothing.

The *Luftpanzer* was gone.

Jack tried to blink the tracers from his eyes, sure that some kind of dark magic had been at work here. As the radio chatter erupted with unsettled questions and observations from the other pilots, Jack found himself throttling down and heading back to the harbor. *It's not possible,* he thought. *It simply couldn't be.*

# # #

As the tropical sun set over crystal blue water, Jack tarried for a moment at the ladder from the *Daedalus* gondola. Stede Bonnet stood on the dock nearby, arms folded across his chest, unsure what to say.

"I don't know how they disappeared or where they went," Jack said, "but we'll find them."

Stede nodded. "I have a town to help rebuild, but we'll be along in due time."

"Thank you, old friend," Jack said, waving from the ladder.

Stede called after him. "If your foe can make a zeppelin disappear, you'll need all the help you can get."

- Chapter 8 -

Captain Ecke paced the bridge deck of the *Luftpanzer*, incensed at the diversion from their primary mission to bomb a small, tropical village full of innocent people. Especially one which had the protection of a sky pirate squadron. It was damned sloppy. What was Maria's endgame? Ecke glanced at her exhausted form crumpled on the cold deck plates. He decided to bide his time and play a good little soldier until this mission was finished, then put in an official request for reassignment.

"Are we away?" he asked the navigator.

"We have cleared West End, *mein Kapitän*."

Ecke looked at Maria on the floor. He knew he didn't want to personally be the one to help her up. "What is Maria's condition?"

A crewman standing by stared forward under his naval cap. "*Ich weiss nicht, Kapitän.*"

Captain Ecke turned to look out the huge panel of forward windows.

"The cloaking spell must have been an incredible strain on her," he deduced. "Take her to her stateroom."

The crewman clicked his heels together and saluted. "*Jawohl, mein Kapitän.*"

As the young man bent to assist Maria, she whirled around, clutching him by the throat.

"NO!" she growled. "I'll be fine."

As she stood, Ecke could see the price she had paid for the magic to make the ship disappear. Her face was gaunt, almost mummified looking, her once-raven hair now stringy and white.

He let out an audible gasp. "Maria! Your face! What has happened to you?"

Maria peered at him through feral slits, a skeletal grin on her thin face. "Why, nothing, *mein Kapitän,*" she rasped, still gripping the crewman by the throat. The young man began to choke and gag, struggling for breath as she clutched his windpipe with bony talons. "Nothing at all..."

As Ecke watched, the color drained from the crewman's cheeks. His eyes rolled back in his head, and his skin collapsed in on itself. He looked like a time-lapse film of a decaying animal, and as his life force ebbed from his body, Maria appeared plump-cheeked and refreshed. Her hair saturated with its previous black color, and her hands—pale though they were—returned to their toned and manicured state.

"*Mein Gott!*" Ecke remarked as Maria released her grip and let the crewman slump to the floor, quite dead.

"In fact," Maria continued, "I've never felt better."

Ecke found himself in a moral quandary, disposable as he knew Silver Star soldiers were meant to be. "Maria..." he stammered. "The crewman... you... you killed him."

Maria smiled at him and he felt sick. "No, Ecke," she corrected softly. "I merely drained his youth."

As she passed Captain Ecke on her way off the bridge, she added, "It was his advanced age that killed him."

# # #

The *Daedalus* hovered at anchor, tethered to a lavish sailing yacht just off Basse Tene, on the southern coast of Tortuga. It had taken a full day to track down the Frenchman, even with the network of radio operators at Edison's command. But he just happened to be on what he called a "working holiday" in Haiti, and was happy to meet with AEGIS' first airship reconnaissance crew.

The sun had set an hour ago, and the local bulldog bats were skimming the shallow waters of the bay for fish. A few lights were visible from the island, but the anchorage was far from most nautical traffic. In centuries past, Tortuga was simultaneously a pirate haven and the site of a great Utopian social experiment. Now it was a territory of Haiti, and mostly produced sugar cane and coffee for export.

The yacht was white with polished teak and brass appointments. She was registered out of Martinique, and her name was *Mon Dieu*. And anyone who knew the Frenchman might have an idea as to why that was funny.

Louis Lambeau was in his forties, and had been kicked so often by life that it was really no wonder he was who he was. Orphan, ex-street urchin, ex-convict, ex-Legion, ex-mercenary. Current smuggler and grave robber. Unrepentant capitalist, hedonist and atheist, in that order. Louis worshiped money far more than art, and wine, and beautiful young men. After all, he figured, money could ultimately purchase all three. Money had purchased the yacht. Naming her *My God* was really the only possible choice.

Jack and Doc rested on red crushed velvet cushions in the boat's main saloon. Louis had set out a champagne service with a sterling silver ice bucket and crystal glasses. He was the very picture of cosmopolitan in his white cotton suit, slicked hair and dark pencil mustache. A white Panama hat hung on the coat tree by the entry stairs. As much as Louis loved money, the only jewelry he wore was a small signet ring with the French Foreign Legion flag etched on the face, worn on his right pinky. Jack noticed the ring as Louis poured three glasses of bubbly, handing two to his guests.

Doc broke the silence first. "Thank you so much for meeting with us, Mr. Lambeau."

Louis smiled and winked at her. "Ze pleasure is mine, Madame," he replied in accented English. He raised his sparkling glass in a toast. "To Colonel Starr," he offered. "An officer, a gentleman, and my good friend."

The three clinked glasses together, Jack offering a solemn, "Hear, hear."

Louis turned to sit across from his two visitors. "I was most distressed to hear of his... assassination at ze hands of *Monsieur diabolique* Crowley."

Doc sat forward, the bubbles from the champagne making her nose itch. "I know you were Dirk's friend, Louis," she said earnestly. "He always spoke very highly of you. And that is why we called you."

Jack knocked back the champagne in one shot, much to his host's chagrin. "We need your assistance, Mr. Lambeau," he said. "And your discretion."

Louis raised an eyebrow. *This could prove*

interesting, he thought. "But of course, Monsieur," he said innocently. "Anything in my power."

Doc set her glass aside and started with a tentative approach. "We know that in your line of work, you sometimes come across certain... artifacts."

Jack leaned back on the crushed velvet settee and frowned. Doc was talking like a flippin' G-man. There was no reason for delicacy here. He'd heard all about Lambeau's background and he struck Jack as a no-nonsense guy.

A smile crept across the right side of Louis' face, taking his thin mustache for a ride. "I have sometimes trafficked in ze rare and mysterious object, *oui.*"

Jack cut to the chase. "We're looking for a lost Spanish artifact. Early 16th century. The Cross of Cadiz. Have you heard of it?"

Doc gave Jack a sideways glance, and Louis rubbed his jaw.

"Zat depends, *Capitaine* Jack..."

Doc leaned forward to look at the Frenchman. "We are authorized to wire ten thousand U.S. dollars if you help us secure the artifact."

There was an awkward silence, as Louis weighed the offer.

"Plus expenses," Doc added.

Louis smiled broadly. "Ah, Madame, I sink

we can do business."

# # #

The tiny outboard engine rattled and sputtered rhythmically, pushing the twenty-foot wooden launch along the Rivière Mapou inland toward the tropical jungles and coffee plantations of central Haiti. Louis handled the tiller, shaded from the relentless sun by his white Panama hat. Doc and Jack had left their flight leathers back on the *Daedalus*, if only because wearing anything non-porous on one's head in this heat was a good way to get sunstroke. Rolled shirtsleeves, jodhpurs and boots were the order of the day. Deadeye had kept his trousers, boots and puttees, but had discarded his Army fatigue jacket in favor of a simple cotton shirt which also had the sleeves pushed up. They'd left Rivets and Duke back on the ship to keep an ear on the radio chatter and an eye on the horizon. If the *Luftpanzer* appeared, they were to retreat to any safe harbor and report back to Edison at once.

Meanwhile, the small boat puttered up the Mapou, the water dark green and gray with algae, sediment and detritus. Jack cataloged at least a dozen new assaults on his olfactory system, and watched sleek black crocodiles breach the surface to stare at them with knobby eyes. An endless blanket of green vegetation spread out before them, crisscrossed by the shimmering river, its stillness disturbed only by the call of tropical birds and the sputtering outboard motor.

After two miles of winding river through jungle and plantation, Jack finally spoke.

"Where is it, exactly?"

Louis was matter-of-fact. "There is a *Vodou bokor* who runs a cane plantation out of an old Spanish fort, about six kilometers up river. His name is Oba, and he is said to be served by a hundred *zombis*. If anyone has knowledge of the Cross of Cadiz, it is Oba."

Deadeye was intrigued. "What's a *zombi*?" he asked.

Louis explained as he would the rules of poker. "They say it is someone raised from the dead and bound to ze *Vodou bokor*."

Jack frowned. "Sounds like a raw deal to me," he muttered.

"It is," Doc assured him. "They're aware every moment. They can feel pain and fear, and can do nothing but obey the *bokor* who created them."

"It is a living hell, *Capitaine* Jack," Louis assured him, as he negotiated a bend in the river.

Jack looked at Doc. "Are we gonna be okay with this Oba fella?"

"Yes," Doc assured him. "As long as we're

respectful."

"I'm respectful," Jack insisted.

Doc smiled at him and blotted a bead of sweat from his nose with her bandanna.

# # #

Within the cold, stone walls of the ancient, abandoned Spanish outpost, the *Vodou* sorcerer Oba sat on a carved chair, golden goblet in hand. Legend put his age somewhere over 300, but in reality he was a descendant of another Oba who plied his mystical trade during the golden age of Caribbean piracy. He wore a top hat from the past century, festooned with animal bones and feathers. A brocade waistcoat and short pantaloons were his only other clothing. His face and body were painted in skeletal designs which contrasted with his dark Caribbean skin. Sipping from his golden chalice—a trophy from an age-old pirate raid—his furrowed brow betrayed troubled thoughts. The zombi slave tending the cook fire on the hearth suddenly turned to glance at the doorway, and Oba knew he wasn't alone. It became strangely cold in the room; an unnatural cold caused not by a river breeze through the open windows, but by dark magic in the hands of an intruder.

"You must be the sorcerer, Oba," Maria

Blutig said as she entered the room with two Silver Star commandos, each armed with an MP18 submachine gun. "Just the man I want to talk to." She held in her hand a four-foot-long staff of lacquered ebony and gold, the relief of a cobra coiled around it, culminating in the serpent's head at the top, complete with jeweled eyes. "Commandos, flank me and let no one pass."

"*Jawohl,*" they answered. Bolts on guns were ratcheted back and released.

Oba wasn't used to visitors in general, and he certainly wasn't happy about these uniformed, Imperial-looking Germans invading his midday meal.

"Who dares trespass in *Cerro de la Mentira,* the home of Oba?" The *bokor* rose threateningly and stood clutching a wand made of animal bones, the skull of a human infant at the top. "Who risks the wrath of *Baron Samedi, Maman Brigitte* and all the *loa?*"

"*RA-HOOR-KHUIT!*" Maria chanted, invoking the cobra-headed staff, whose eyes began to glow with unearthly power.

Oba brandished his wand, spittle flying as he cursed. "*Baron Samedi,* let your wrath be upon the intruders!"

Maria stood fast, staff raised in defiance. "*BES-NA-MAUT! TA-NECH!*"

Oba's curse, "Death be upon you!" echoed

through the hall. His arm flew out and directed the wand at the trio in his doorway, and a
swirling, vaporous fog erupted from the floor
in a straight line, spirit tendrils pulling at the
soldiers as they screamed in agony. Maria,
shielded by the staff, watched as Oba's spell
began to rend and crush her commandos,
compacting them in a series of grotesque *pops*
and *cracks*.

Resolved to have her vengeance, Maria
surged forward with pure malevolence. The cobra's eyes emitted a beam of red energy, which
caught Oba like prey in a car's headlights. Every nerve ignited in brutal pain and he sank to
his knees, gasping for breath that never came.

Maria stood over him triumphantly, eyes
savage and ecstatic. "To answer your question,
Oba," she purred. "I am your doom."

- Chapter 9 -

Louis steered the small boat to a ramshackle dock at the bottom of a terraced rise and tied up. He would watch for trouble and be able to go for help if needed. Jack and Doc checked their sidearms, and Deadeye loaded his Winchester carbine. Then the three of them stepped onto the dock and made their way to the path which cut upward through a lush, green hillside to the ruins of the Spanish fort.

The place was known to history as *Cerro de la Mentira,* or "Deception Hill", a name whose origins were lost in time long before its ruins had been claimed by the *bokors* in Oba's line. Originally a Spanish military garrison and prison, the fort was the staging ground for enforcement of severe Spanish laws in the 16th and 17th centuries, and reprisals against locals who had the nerve to question said laws. Now weather-beaten, with sagging outer walls, the old fort resembled the gnarled hand of an aged man reaching out of the cliff side toward the sky.

Along the path, the party spotted several

groups of people wandering aimlessly within the rows of coffee shrubs, and Jack was filled instantly with a looming dread. Their eyes were white and they stared blankly ahead, unblinking. They wore simple homespun clothes —all ragged and torn from use. Not one head turned to greet the trio as they trod up the path into the shadow of the fort.

"Are these the *zombis* Louis told us about?" Jack asked as they traversed the milling human herd.

Doc nodded. "They seem docile enough," she said. "But let's not disturb them, just the same."

Deadeye clutched the lever of the Winchester in battle-forged readiness. "I'm for that plan," he deadpanned.

They wove through a number of blank stares and ragged bodies as they made their way to the outer gate, only to find that the left side had been pried off its hinges and lay to the side of the courtyard. Another pair of *zombis* trudged randomly around the garden, slowly going nowhere at all. Jack led Doc and Deadeye through the open front doorway, and he immediately knew someone else had been there before them. Jack shucked both .45s from their holsters, which signaled Doc to follow suit with her revolver. Deadeye took it as permission to ready the Winchester, which he braced to his shoulder.

The fort was ancient and dank, and smelled like a curious mixture of coffee, urine, sweat and sulfur. Even the heat of the noon-day sun outside couldn't penetrate the thick stone walls of the Spanish garrison. It remained at least twenty degrees cooler inside.

Jack led the way, cautiously leading with his twin pistols. Doc followed, her own pistol at the ready, lodestone dangling from the leather string around her neck. Deadeye brought up the rear, scanning down the barrel sights of the carbine. They searched the ground floor one chamber at a time, bypassing a curved stairway down to the prison area. The heavy oak doors to the great hall were ajar, and Jack waved his friends back while he peered through the gap between them.

He stepped in, pistols in outstretched hands to the left and right, scanning the room with sun-blind eyes. Four roughly human-sized shapes lay in crumpled heaps on the cold stone.

"Doc!" he hailed. "Get in here!"

Doc followed him into the room. She immediately recognized the smoldering remains of two of the shapes.

"Silver Star commandos," she gasped.

Jack looked over his shoulder at the doorway. "Deadeye, take a look around upstairs. See if they left any more clues."

"Affirmative," said Deadeye, and he disappeared up the main stairwell.

Jack entered the center of the room and tried to let his eyes adjust to the dim light. Doc was already checking the bodies. The two commandos were little more than piles of wet ash and uniforms. The body of a female *zombi*, her throat cut, lay near the hearth.

Then Jack saw the slightest movement from the last body and he rushed to check it out.

"Oh no," he said, holstering his guns.

Doc rushed to his side. "Is that Oba?" she asked, kneeling to the floor and rolling the figure over into her lap.

It was indeed the *Vodou bokor*, painted markings smeared with his own blood. He'd been stabbed through the heart. His breath came and went as a labored wheeze. His eyes searched for Doc's, and when they met, he reached for the lodestone around her neck. Although startled at first, Doc let him continue, wishing she could alleviate his pain.

"Av... avenge..." he pleaded through dry, chapped lips.

Then his head rolled back and he lost consciousness, hand still clutching the lodestone, which leaked spectral light through his dark fingertips. When at last he released it and slipped away into death, the stone shone a bright ice blue and almost hummed with the energy infused in it.

"He's dead," Doc announced.

But Jack was transfixed on the stone. "Look, Doc! It's glowing like crazy!"

Doc let Oba's body slump back to the floor. She undid the strap of the lodestone from around her neck and let it hang. The stone twisted back and forth, finally becoming still as it angled toward the cook hearth. "Over there," she pointed. "It's the hearth."

Jack went to the hearth and gently rolled the dead *zombi* away. As he did so, he noticed the corner tile jiggle beneath the weight. He knelt, trying to pry it loose. Doc went to his side and fanned dust and cooking debris away. He flipped the tile over, revealing a simple, folded piece of tanned leather.

Doc opened the leather with eyes wide. "It's a map!"

Jack led her to an exterior window and pulled the burlap curtain aside to let some light in. Together they pored over what appeared to be a primitive treasure map inked on pig hide.

# # #

Deadeye circled out of the stairwell into a gallery which looked over the entry of the fort on his right, and a line of former officer's quarters on the left. Most were empty, save for the occasional roaming chicken, pecking at the hay-strewn floors. However one room—the centermost with double doors—was padlocked from the outside.

Charlie leaned the Winchester against the wall and took a knee. Fishing his trench knife out of its belt sheath and a metal strip clip from another pouch, he inserted both into the archaic lock and began to wiggle the primitive tumblers into place.

The thick ring sprang open, and Charlie set the old lock down quietly, standing to open the door.

He pulled the right door open with the deep moan of wrought iron hinges, and his eyes grew wide.

The room was full of wooden crates, each stenciled with the words *ACHTUNG - EXPLO-SIVE*. Thick cord fuses bound with tape extended upward to the ceiling and across to the door. The door Charlie had just opened, triggering a chemical reaction in the glass bulb set to go off if anyone attempted a breach.

Deadeye heard the hiss of multiple fuses burning, and he knew they didn't have much time. He grabbed the Winchester and sprinted for the stairway.

# # #

Maria stormed up the gantry to the *Luft-panzer* radio room, furious.

Furious at Oba's stoicism. Furious at her own failure to acquire the cross or any fresh clues as to its whereabouts. The radio officer could hear her coming outside the door, and readied himself for a quick break while Maria spoke with headquarters. He was standing when she entered, bowing slightly as he offered her the headset. Then he disappeared into the hallway, leaving Maria in private.

"Blutig," she signaled.

"Maria," came a reedy voice tinged with a posh English accent from across the wireless. "I need you to abort the current mission and bring your complement to the following coordinates: 2 degrees, 6 hours, 22.6 minutes north by 63 degrees, 12 hours, 10.5 minutes west."

"But Master," Maria protested. "The Cross of Cadiz was almost within our grasp. I just need a few more days..."

"You do not have days to spend, Maria," said the voice. "Your failure to procure the Cross of Cadiz has cost soldiers and material. And your bombing of West End accomplished nothing."

"But we had the *Daedalus*—"

"I will not tolerate excuses and I will not tolerate insubordination!" Crowley's anger buzzed into her ear like angry hornets. "Your vanity and selfishness almost cost the *Luft-panzer*! You will listen to me and you will obey, or you will be punished."

His words seared into her skull and they stung. Her eyes welled up with tears but she willed them dry.

"Yes, Master."

Suddenly the voice on the radio was calm. "Very good, Maria. We do not look backward, do we?"

Maria sighed, "No, Master."

"No indeed. We look forward. Your presence is required here, for the summoning."

"Master, with respect," Maria said through clenched teeth. "The Cross—"

"The Cross will soon be in the hands of the *Daedalus* crew."

Maria fumed. It wasn't like Crowley to abort an important project like this.

"We cannot just walk away..."

"Oh but you are walking away," Crowley maintained. "But that does not mean the Cross of Cadiz will remain in the possession of our enemy."

Maria swallowed dryly. While she respected Crowley's foresight to stand back and let the *Daedalus* crew do the hard work in retrieving the artifact, he was going to send someone else—another team—to steal it back. She desperately wanted to be the one to do it.

"Please, Master..."

"You will do as I say, Maria, or bear the consequences." The voice was calm, matter-of-fact, and those qualities more than the words themselves sent a chill down her spine.

Maria felt her heart thud deeply within her chest. This was a blow to her pride, but Maria had always played the long game. If Crowley needed her, she would play the good soldier. She would obey.

"Acknowledged," she told him, clamping her eyes tight with shame.

"Very well," buzzed the response. "We will expect you in thirty-six hours, no later. Over and out."

# # #

Jack and Doc stood by the window in the great hall, a warm breeze drifting in from the river valley below. Although they were technically on the ground floor, the fort itself sprouted from the cliff sixty feet above the Mapou. They scanned the leather map for clues.

Jack pointed at one corner. "The picture on the legend appears to be..."

"A jeweled cross," Doc finished, smiling.

Jack chuckled. "Well I'll be darned." He traced the aged ink line in a curious puzzle piece shape. "What's this, here?"

"Coast line," said Doc. "It's not labeled. We'll have to match it to the charts, or find a local who knows the islands."

"Perhaps Louis would know."

"And if he doesn't, he knows someone who would."

Then Deadeye burst into the room at full speed. "No time to explain!" he warned. "We need to go! Now!"

- Chapter 10 -

The fort exploded in a sudden, almost pyroclastic display. The cliff side shook as the old fort collapsed on itself and its top half slid into the river. The sky became dark with smoke, and the water below churned with stones and human remains.

Louis watched from the dock and his heart sank. "*Sacré bleu*," he whispered, quickly untying the boat and pushing away from the dock. If nothing else, he would retrieve the bodies of his comrades and return them to AEGIS officials. He felt it was the least he could do.

Merde, he cursed to himself. *That is no way to think. They may be yet be alive and in need of aid.*

Then the outboard engine sputtered to life and Louis sped toward the river bend.

Doc felt her stomach leap into her throat as she plummeted into the river from sixty feet up. She caught glimpses of Jack and Deadeye as she fell, then her world was completely dark and wet, and her mouth was full of algae. Bubbles cascaded from her throat and nose as she spat out the foul-tasting vegetation. She kicked for the surface, Deadeye clutching the rear strap of her suspenders as he helped her upward.

The small boat was just yards away, and Louis was ready to help haul them out of the brackish river. Deadeye pushed Doc toward Louis' outstretched arms. She was just clearing the side when her eyes nervously scanned the water and she made a terrible realization.

"Where's Jack??"

Jack could only see a swirl of green vegetation and bubbles as he tried to get to the river's surface. But a great black shadow filled his limited vision and the saltwater crocodile turned and bolted right for him. The reptile hit Jack like a twenty-foot-long locomotive, and the only thing that saved him were the words of a French pilot he'd met during the war—a fellow who had done some big game hunting in the Congo. He recalled that, although a crocodile had a deadly, crushing downward bite, the muscles for opening its mouth were relatively weak.

His lungs already burning for air, Jack hugged the beast underneath its massive belly and unfastened his suspenders, quickly wrapping them around its snout a few times. Then he kicked away and swam for the surface.

The croc was loose in moments, shedding the makeshift muzzle and aiming for Jack again. All Jack could see among the murky green-black water was the enormous silhouette looming under him and the long jaws opening under his feet. Unwilling to have survived a world war, Italian fascists and an exploding Spanish fort, only to become lunch for a prehistoric throwback, Jack kicked a booted leg at the beast's head—just as it was perforated by an aluminum harpoon. The projectile hit the croc between the eyes, and the bubbling water churned deep crimson with blood.

Jack didn't feel his head break the surface, but suddenly he was in the light, being hauled into the small motorboat by two sets of strong hands. He coughed up brackish water and rolled into the bottom, turning over. As he looked up, clearing the muck from his eyes, he could see Louis standing amidships, tracking something underwater with a spear gun. The bloated corpse of the giant reptile bobbed to the surface and rolled over in the water, as Deadeye slapped his back and Doc made sure there were no other obstructions in his airway and field of vision.

"Holy..." Jack stammered. "B-big croc!"

Louis turned toward the engine at the rear of the small boat and stowed the speargun beneath his seat. "Close to twenty feet," he observed.

"That was an amazing shot, Louis. Thank you," Jack said.

"*Merci, mon ami,*" Louie smiled. "Many years of hunting big game."

Deadeye clapped one final had on Jack's shoulder. "Close one, Cap."

Jack nodded. That was an understatement. He found Doc on the opposite seat.

"Still got the map?" he asked.

She produced a sopping folded piece of leather. "Right here."

Louis peered over Doc's shoulder. "May I see it?"

Doc unfolded the map and laid it out onto the sunbaked seat in the open boat.

Louis rubbed his jaw, squinting at the details. "Ah, yes," he nodded. "About five kilometers off Monte Cristi, in the Dominican Republic. There are several wrecks in that area."

Doc squinted at the florid Spanish calligraphy. "This specifies the *Nuestra Señora de la salvación,*" she pointed out.

Jack set his jaw. "Then that's where we're going. We can only hope the Silver Star didn't get the wreck's location from Oba."

Louis steered the boat back down the river whence they came, as Jack watched the flames and billowing smoke dance in the shell of the old Spanish fortress.

# # #

Louis brought Jack, Doc and Deadeye back to the *Daedalus*, and sailed his yacht to Cap Haïtien, where he bought a few drinks, asked a few questions, and hired a salvage crew that very night to take them out to the wreck. The ship was perhaps 20 years old, complete with rusty welds and an asthmatic diesel engine. Her name was *L'arlequin* and she was held together with baling wire and profanity. The following day found them anchored near a reef miles from the nearest port, *Daedalus* flying a patrol route above.

Jack shrugged his shoulders in the heavy confines of the treated canvas dive suit. It was fitted with buckles and straps and weights, and sealed at the boots, gloves and collar. A heavy brass helmet with glass portholes would be fitted onto the yoke and have air pumped into it via one of two sputtering compressors on the aft deck.

Doc smiled at him, swimming inside her own diving suit and looking like a little girl playing dress-up in adult clothes.

A crew of ten swarthy men—mostly shirt-less and running the gamut of adjectives from sweaty to emaciated to drunk—roamed the decks, tending to various stations and chores. Their chatter was a hodge-podge of French and Creole and there might have been a hundred teeth among the lot of them. Jack couldn't have imagined a shadier-looking bunch outside of a pirate novel.

Louis double-checked the air hoses running from the compressors to the matching dive helmets, as Jack listened to a report from the portable two-way wireless set they'd taken aboard the salvage vessel to communicate with the *Daedalus*.

"Patrol complete, Cap," said Rivets over the speaker. "You're all clear."

Doc leaned in and Jack keyed the *TALK* button on the handset for her. "You sure there's no sign of the *Luftpanzer*?" she asked.

Duke's voice crackled over the tiny speaker coil. "We've done several sweeps with the radio detector at altitude," he explained. "The only thing matching the *Luftpanzer*'s radio signature is headed south-southeast in a hurry."

"Affirmative," said Jack. "Captain out."

"I wonder what they know," Doc mused.

Jack signaled Louis for help with the dive helmet. "We'll find out after we find the artifact," he said.

Louis hefted the cumbersome helmet onto Jack's shoulders with his help, explaining as they worked. "I will stay on ze radio with *Daedalus* while you are below. Zese men will keep your air flowing and pull you up when you tug three times on ze tether."

Jack's helmet was sealed down, followed by Doc's. Each nodded at Louis when they felt the compressed air fill the chamber. Giving each other an OK sign, they trudged down the ship's ladder and into the depths.

"*Bonne chance, Capitaine*," Louis saluted as the pair disappeared in a fountain of bubbles.

Only a dozen feet down, the reef was alive with a rainbow of color. Striped tropical fish darted in schools from coral branch to coral branch. Blood-red seaweed fronds and brilliant yellow tube sponges waved gently in the current. A spotted moray eel peeked out from its lair among the rocks and anemones, "sniffing" the water with its open mouth, then disappeared.

The reef itself ran north-south, gently sloping away into deeper waters to the west. If *Our Lady of Salvation* had encountered this jagged reef in calm seas—let alone a storm—it would not have gone well for her. The wreck would be close by, in those deeper waters. As their air hoses and tether lines payed out behind them, the two divers hopped slowly from the reef to the white sand below. Jack led the way with a sealed lantern, Doc following with the lodestone held out in front of her. She thrilled to the alien world laid out before them.

At thirty feet, the sunlight from above was

so diffuse as to appear like evening. A school of blue tang whisked past them, fleeing a reef shark prowling above. The sand here was dusty white and kicked up into small clouds around the divers' feet. A pair of stingrays erupted from the sea floor and flapped away into the dark. The ground continued to slope down, toward a field of seagrass which waved lazily before them.

As they hit sixty feet, Jack's lantern beam was suddenly interrupted by a huge shape resting between the grassy sea floor and a small mountain of rocks which extended back to the main reef. The *Nuestra Señora de la salvación* lay on her belly, in remarkable condition for her age, save for the giant tear in her keel and almost four centuries' worth of barnacle growth. There was no doubt as to what had sunk her. A larger question was how she hadn't been completely torn in half, given the extent of the damage. Jack's light played across the Spanish galleon's elaborately carved stern, and Doc noted the name. This was indeed the ship. The lodestone glowed with a faint blue light, urging Doc toward the captain's cabin.

They approached the stern, and Doc noticed a wide hole where ornate leaded glass once enclosed the aft cabin—the cabin where the captain slept and the ship's officers ate their meals. She was about to step through when Jack caught her arm and had her pause while he peered inside with the lantern. The cabin was the only structure still in an approximation of its original shape. The floorboards were dusted with sand and sediment, seagrass reaching through the seams. An oak table lay on its side in the corner, missing a leg. Various tarnished silver goblets and utensils were scattered about, and a small crab skittered away from the light, disappearing under the cabin door. The room was otherwise unoccupied.

Giving Doc a thumbs up, Jack held out his hand to help her inside. She stepped up into the wreck, her weighted boots kicking up the dusty sand from the floor. Jack followed, clipping the lantern to a hook on his weight belt and unhooking a crowbar from the same place. They scanned the room's interior. Outside, a sea turtle glided past the hole where the windows used to be.

Doc held the lodestone out, letting it hang from its leather strap. She knew after this trip she'd have to replace the leather with a proper metal chain, but something that wouldn't interfere with its magnetic properties. The stone pulsed with bright blue light, one end pointing and pulling toward the corner of the room where the table had overturned. She waved Jack over and pointed toward the heavy old table.

Jack re-secured the crowbar to his belt and grasped the table with both hands, pulling it backwards with every ounce of strength he could muster. It came away far easier than he'd expected, and he stumbled back with most of it.

The skeletal remains of someone Doc presumed to be the captain had been trapped under the table for four centuries. The body had been picked clean by scavenging fish, but the bones had grown a new layer of barnacle and sponge. A tiny gray-green crab appeared from the eye socket of the skull and quickly darted back inside.

Jack peered over Doc's shoulder and pointed to an object the late captain had been holding when the ship went down those many years ago. An iron box, roughly 24 inches long and 10 wide, wrapped in heavy chain, sat under a skeletal hand with a missing index finger and an enormous emerald ring sitting loose on the pinky.

Doc knelt on the dusty floor and gently pulled the box from the captain's grasp. She turned, the lodestone glowing brightly and almost magnetically attached to the box. Tucking the lodestone away, Doc placed the iron box on the floor and signaled Jack to use the crowbar.

Jack unhooked the crowbar from his belt and found an especially weak point in one of the rusted chain links. A simple twist popped the link open and Doc was able to do the rest. The chain fell away and the lid opened to reveal the decayed velvet-lined home of a beautiful gold cross, beset with large jewels in early Baroque Spanish style.

This had to be it. They'd found the Cross of Cadiz.

Jack knelt across from Doc and looked at her. He could see her look of abject excitement in the lantern light, moments before a giant red tentacle coiled around her waist and pulled her backward through the cabin breach.

Without thinking twice, Jack grabbed the cross from the iron box and clambered out of the hole in the stern.

He could see Doc coiled in what appeared to be the arm of a gigantic octopus of some kind. Glaring out of the crevice in the ship's midsection was a single yellow eye, which became the spongy brick red body of the creature as it oozed out from its hiding place. Its body was perhaps thirty feet long from the tip of its bulbous head to its snapping beak, with tentacles twice as long.

Spanish sailors had told tales of el *Diablo del Mar*, the Devil of the Sea, a creature that hid among the reefs and would pick apart foundering ships, dragging sailors down to feed upon them. Jack read the stories as a child, but always assumed them to be the colorful folklore of a simpler time. Yet here he was, face to face with just such a creature, a day after encountering *Vodoun zombis*, escaping an exploding Spanish fort, and wrestling a saltwater crocodile.

With his dive knife in one hand and the Cross of Cadiz in the other, Jack hopped through the water like a man on the surface of the Moon. Doc had freed her own knife and was slicing at the tentacle coiled around her. She could see the scars of previous encounters running like hash-marks down the length of each flexing red arm, and knew that hacking at it with an eight-inch blade probably wouldn't do much good. Still, it was the only weapon she had.

Jack leaped up onto the raised aftercastle where a mast had once stood proud and sturdy, but had been subsumed by the reef. The creature was pulling Doc toward its body, most likely with the intent to devour her in its enormous beaked maw.

He pulled some slack in his air hose, aimed himself toward the giant eye and pushed off.

- Chapter 11 -

The air compressors chugged dutifully as the hose and tethers unspooled off the back of the salvage ship. Louis paced the deck, frowning in worry. He didn't notice the crewman with the four-pointed star tattooed on his wrist until the man had slashed the air hoses with a fishing knife.

Compressed air began to hiss from the severed lines, and Louis turned to face the saboteur, aghast. The man glared at him from savage eyes under a receding brown hairline, hunching into a fighting stance.

"What have you done??" he accused. "Zey will die without air!"

The man simply thrust his knife at Louis' throat, and the Frenchman was forced to duck away. Pivoting on his right foot, he knocked the knife from his assailant's hand, grabbing the back of his striped shirt and tripping him toward the stern rail. The man impacted the railing with a huff, then rolled and let fly with a random left cross. The punch missed Louis by several inches. Louis was far more accurate with his. He felt the man's jaw pop out of position as the rest of him sailed over the railing and into the water.

# # #

Jack felt the tentacle wrap tightly around his leg as he neared the leviathan's head. He slashed at it with the dive knife, doing negligible damage as he felt his lungs begin to burn. He gasped a breath that was stale and heavy and his heart raced with a rising dread as water began to seep into the heavy helmet.

Someone had cut their hoses.

Doc frantically pulled at the arm wrapped around her, flailing her arms in panic as her air failed. If Jack had been alone on this venture, he might have been tempted to let nature play out, but he refused to let Doc become a meal on his watch.

Then he noticed the gold of the Cross of Cadiz begin to take on a brighter hue. He thought perhaps it was his oxygen-deprived brain hallucinating, but soon the object had built up a significant glare—to the point that Jack couldn't look at it—and with it an unearthly hum. Then there was an explosion of light, like a thousand white phosphorus grenades going off simultaneously, accompanied by a piercing screech like high-volume feedback, and suddenly they were free.

The gigantic cephalopod retreated into its dark hole in the ship, and Jack grasped blindly through the water. Somehow he found Doc's dive suit, dropped both weight belts and pushed for the surface.

As they swam, they fumbled with straps, kicking away the weighted shoes, the heavy gloves, and the brass helmets.

Jack pulled through the water with one hand grasping the cross, the other clutching Doc. He would not let her die. Damn it, not today. Not now.

The Devil of the Sea quickly regrouped from its surprise and erupted from the shipwreck, angrier than before. Sixty-foot tentacles snaked through the water, reaching toward the surface as the two exhausted divers climbed the volume of water, struggling for breath.

Come on, Doc! Jack thought. *Swim!*

Then they broke the water's surface, gasping and choking, filling their lungs with fresh air. Still some fifty feet away, they began to crawl for the boat's ladder as Louis rallied them closer.

Jack felt a heavy shape brush along his side as they swam with every bit of strength they could muster. It was either a giant octopus tentacle or a reef shark, and he didn't care to know which. He kept swimming, pushing Doc through the water as she tried to reach the boat. Doc made the ladder first, just as Jack was pulled under. She turned to call out, but he was gone.

Then the water lit up from below and there was an enormous splash from the underwater explosion.

A second explosion, and a third, erupted from the ocean surface.

Jack popped up and scampered over the ladder onto the aft deck of the salvage boat, looking up to see the *Daedalus* soaring along at low altitude.

Duke sat in the open side door, dropping grenades into the water. "Tally ho, boys!" he cried. "Calamari for supper, eh wot?"

Jack saluted as the airship passed overhead. "Good way to cover our exit," he chuckled.

Louis and Doc helped Jack to his feet. Louis was effusive in his apology.

"I am so sorry, *mon amis*, zere was a saboteur. He cut your hoses, but I knocked him overboard."

Jack turned to look out over the water. "Where is he?"

Louis handed Jack his binoculars. Jack scanned the ocean surface, finally catching the shape of a person swimming away from the salvage boat. Panning the field glasses, Jack found a small, unmanned motorboat anchored some 200 years away to the south.

"Ah," he said. "He's headed for that boat in the distance."

As he watched through the binoculars, Jack saw a familiar red tentacle coil around the swimming man, then he was gone, dragged beneath the waves.

Well, Jack thought, *it looks like the beast will feed after all.*

Louis patted Jack on the shoulder. His dive suit was torn and dirty, and he looked funny with the rubber helmet yoke over his collar and no boots on. "Good to see ze expedition was a success, non? Now to get the cross to safety."

"Uh, Jack?" Doc chimed.

Jack and Louis turned to see the entire crew assembled on the stern deck, holding them at gunpoint.

Jack sighed. Was this for real?

The ringleader of the pirates, a Creole with rotten teeth and a stained bandanna, stepped forward, aiming a Mauser pistol at Jack. "The cross is worth far more than your promised wages, Lambeau," he explained. "Give it to us and we won't shoot you."

"That's nice of ya," Jack snarled.

The gunman snickered back at him. "We'll

just let you swim for it," he said. "I'm sure your airship will rescue you before *El Diablo del Mar* returns."

Jack's eyes narrowed. This day had already taken a toll on his nerves and his patience, and he was more than ready to take it out on these jokers. He'd already judged them to be opportunists rather than experienced brigands, but this would be risky just the same. "If you want it," he grinned, "CATCH!"

Then he hurled the cross high into the air. All crewman eyes followed. The aft deck was suddenly a confused, writhing mass of grasping arms and punching fists and shouting. Pistols skittered across the deck planks as punches flew, Jack and Louis each sending a pair of pirates to the floor. Doc leaped into the air and came down with the cross, while Jack grabbed the Mauser from the pirate leader and waved him to a corner of the deck. The brawl was over as soon as it had begun.

"That's right," he barked, "get 'em up, you cretins!"

An aluminum chain ladder dropped to the deck, and the *Daedalus* came in low. Deadeye sat in the gondola side door, Winchester trained on the crew.

"Looks like I'm just in time," he quipped.

Jack shouted over the electric whine of the engine turbines. "Charlie, get Doc and Louis aboard. I want to make sure our friends here don't try anything."

Doc dropped the cross inside the front of her dive suit and was up the ladder first. Louis followed.

Jack was about to take his turn when a small object rolled across the deck—a shape Jack immediately recognized as a grenade.

Oh no, he thought.

And then his world was fire and thunder.

- Chapter 12 -

The salvage ship exploded as the grenade blew through the deck and ignited the diesel engine beneath. Smoke billowed from the resulting fire as the vessel tore in half, the screams of burning men silenced as they splashed into the ocean.

Louis grasped an upper rung on the ladder, pulling himself toward the open side door of the gondola. Doc looked down past him, into the smoke and fire, but could see nothing. She scanned the water's surface for any hint that he'd been thrown clear.

Nothing.

The *Daedalus* lifted away from the ship, and the end of the ladder finally cleared the smoke. There, hanging from the bottom rung, was a wet and exhausted Jack McGraw.

Rung over rung he climbed, aching and sore from head to toe. "A giant octopus," he mumbled, "a saboteur, and pirates." Inching his way up the ladder, he decided he hated the pirates most of all.

"Here he comes," said Deadeye, stowing the

Winchester as Jack approached the open door. "Grab his arms."

Doc and Deadeye took Jack by the upper torso and hauled him into the airship while Louis pulled the ladder in and slid the gondola door shut. Jack rolled to the floor and—awkwardly—onto Doc.

Her sparkling green eyes took in his bruised face, which was glistening with seawater and sweat.

"Hi there," she said softly.

Jack grinned. "Did you miss me?"

"I knew you'd make it," Doc smiled back, surprised at the level of relief she felt at his presence.

Deadeye helped his captain off the doctor, and Louis folded his arms proudly by the window.

"On ze bright side, we are ahead ze crew wages and boat hire!" he announced.

"Most importantly," Doc added as she pulled the bulky artifact from her dive suit, "we found the Cross of Cadiz."

# # #

The *Daedalus* headed south-southwest to Port au Prince, where they tied down at the bustling harbor and awaited instructions. Duke had radioed in to AEGIS headquarters en route, and was told to stand by. Word traveled fast through Port au Prince about the airship docked at the harbor, and within minutes of tying down, they'd drawn of crowd of some two hundred locals. A few gawkers were brave enough to approach the ship and touch the aluminum paneling of the gondola before retreating into the crowd. Eventually, the local *gendarmerie* arrived and dispersed the crowd, followed by a platoon of US Marines who posted armed guards at the harbor entry and along the pier to where the *Daedalus* hovered from its mooring cables.

Jack was glad to see American military personnel on the job, although there were disturbing rumors floating around regarding mistreatment of the Haitian populace under the occupation. He hoped it wasn't true, but he'd seen other examples of so-called "gunboat diplomacy", so he wasn't about to discount it.

It was high noon the next day when they got the call on the radio that their contact was available to meet. Jack and Doc accompanied Louis to a small private office above a dress shop on Rue Bonne Foi.

The day was hot and muggy, and ill-maintained motorcars vied with horse buggies and mule carts for possession of the road. The trio —dressed in their lightest traveling clothes and hats—got out of their taxi a block away to throw off potential tails, and negotiated their way across a gauntlet of angry traffic to the opposite side of the street, ducking up a staircase to a second floor balcony. The Cross of Cadiz, wrapped securely in canvas cloth and tied in brown paper, was nestled carefully under Jack's arm.

A small, pale man of fifty, flush-faced and sweating through his shirt, beckoned them into the office and flopped down in a wicker chair behind a rather ornate office desk, atop which sat a nondescript leather valise. Joe Salyer was miserable in the tropical heat, and found he constantly had to remove his round glasses and dry them with a handkerchief because they kept fogging up. "I understand the *Daedalus* crew has been successful in retrieving the Cross of Cadiz," he huffed, fanning himself with a postcard, oblivious to the motorized fan spinning directly overhead.

Jack looked around and could tell this office had been hastily rented. "As promised," he said, placing the parcel on the desk.

Salyer didn't bother to open it. "Mr. Edison sends his sincerest thanks and congratulations," he said. "You've done well, all of you."

Jack shrugged. "All in a day's work, Mr. Salyer."

Doc leaned forward. "But we are anxious to continue our pursuit of the *Luftpanzer*," she urged.

"Indeed," Salyer nodded. Then he noticed Louis and pulled a stuffed envelope out of the leather satchel and pushed it forward on the desk. "As promised, Mr. Lambeau, ten thousand US dollars."

Louis took the envelope. "*Merci.*"

Salyer removed his glasses to clean them again. "And for the *Daedalus* crew, we have some supplies for you. They're being loaded now at the harbor."

After explaining future procedures, Salyer assured Jack and Doc that he would be their primary field contact in the eastern US and Caribbean region. They bid him goodbye and hailed a taxi back to the harbor. None of them happened to spot the well-dressed European businessman in the company of two Haitian bruisers ascend the stairs to the office moments later.

Louis still had to find his way back to Cap Haïtien, where the *Mon Dieu* was docked, but he promised to see Jack and Doc off at the pier.

Jack paid the cabbie and the three walked back to the airship, passing multiple marine sentries on the way. When they arrived at the end of the pier, a crane was lowering the last of several wooden crates onto the dock.

Duke checked boxes on a clipboard manifest. He almost didn't notice the trio approaching.

"Ahoy, Duke!" Jack hailed. "What's in all the boxes?"

Duke looked up and smiled. "Edison sent us some smart uniforms, Captain."

Deadeye pried open the last crate, eyes widening.

"As well as some rather spiffing gadgets and whatnot," Duke added.

Deadeye reached into the crate and produced a rifle which looked as though it had popped out of the garden shed of H.G. Wells. He flipped a switch and a peculiar hum powered on. The Cherokee blinked and lit up, grinning like a kid in an ice cream shop for the first time. "I cannot wait to find out what this does," he said conspiratorially.

Louie turned and shook Jack's hand. "Best of luck in your journey, *Capitaine*," he said. "I remain at your service."

Doc leaned in and kissed the Frenchman's cheek. "Goodbye, Louis."

Louis smiled. "Madame."

"Thanks for your help, Louis," said Jack. "I wish we could stay awhile, or at least give you a lift back to Cap Haïtien, but the *Luftpanzer* is going the opposite direction, and we've got to run."

Louis smiled his devilish smile, bowing as he backed away. "Ah, *mon Capitaine*. I have friends all over Haiti. I am sure I can find someone to give me a ride!"

Then he was gone, and Rivets was admonishing everyone to strip the crates and leave the empties on the pier to conserve weight. Duke hefted several folded garments into the hold. They were royal blue with white piping and had AEGIS and *Daedalus* patches sewn to the sleeves and chest. When Jack had taken off his RAF uniform at the end of the war, he'd sworn never to put on another, but he admitted the new jackets looked good.

Finally, supplies secured, they cast off the dock lines and closed the cargo bay door as the airship rose into the afternoon sky.

# # #

The jungle night was dark and still, with only the slightest dappling of gray indicating a moon above the canopy. Rattan palms and rubber trees thrust their sturdy trunks toward the sky, covered in orchids and epiphytes, surrounded by hanging heliconias. The ground here was wet, swamp-like. It smelled fetid. Not a bird called. Neither an ant nor spider crawled. There were no sounds in the night here.

This was a place of death.

Maria knelt in meditation within a powdered chalk circle, gathering the inner strength necessary for what was to come next. She focused on the solitary black candle at the head of the circle, probing the living memory of this place. A place that had seen natives massacred and conquistadors die of yellow fever. A place once sacred, but which had become a dumping ground—a convenient mass grave—forgotten and left to rot over the centuries.

Her eyes rolled back in her head and Maria shot to her feet, hands outstretched, reaching into the boggy soil, reaching backward in time. The spell consisted only of her power words and her will. It was not intended to be pretty, or even accurate. She simply needed to raise the dead.

A whole lot of dead.

"*Nuit, Hadit, Ra-Hoor-Khuit*," she repeated over and over, reaching out, delving ever deeper into the past, into the soil. She felt her body grow ever lighter and eventually her feet left the ground.

"*Nuit, Hadit, Ra-Hoor-Khuit*."

The swamp began to bubble and swell, tiny mounds erupting through the ground like boils. First a skeletal hand, then an arm, then the remainder of a body crawled out of its resting place, covered in the filth of ages past.

"*Nuit, Hadit, Ra-Hoor-Khuit*."

One, then two, then five, then a dozen. Then two dozen. One by one, they shambled out of the ground and gathered around the clearing.

As Maria's feet returned to the ground within the circle, so to did her eyes return to normal. She gazed out at thirty corpses, both Spanish and indigenous, in various states of decomposition. Corpses now standing upright, waiting for her to command them.

Maria's lips drew into a tight smile.

- Chapter 13 -

Doc determined a total distance of 1,237 miles to the Venezuela-Brazil border, which would take them just shy of 16 hours to complete at a cruising speed of 80 miles per hour. They could cut it down to 13 hours at top speed, maybe 12 with a good tailwind. Unfortunately the *Daedalus* was left fighting a crosswind all the way across the Caribbean Sea, and by the time they hit land, it had already taken them over 8 hours. Jack flew most of that distance, and was exhausted by the time the lights of Caracas were visible beneath them. The crosswind disappeared over Venezuela, and by the time Rivets took his turn at the stick, it was smooth sailing. Jack decided to hit the rack in his quarters, dead to the world for a solid four hours.

When he awoke, the morning light was streaming in through the gondola windows in shades of misty pink, blue and gold. Squinting against the light, Jack stumbled across the main saloon to the galley and began rummaging for something to eat. He found a couple of hard boiled eggs in the cooler, which he paired with a tin of corned beef and a chunky brown oat-and-raisin biscuit which resembled a rectangular cookie, but had the approximate density of a star. He poured a mug of hot coffee from the dedicated electric percolator, and sat down to enjoy his modest feast. He was used to field rations, and these were better by any metric.

Doc poked her head out of the bridge hatch, ducking into the galley. She regarded the haggard captain for a moment. Despite the lack of regular sleep, a steady diet of field rations and mortal danger, and a schedule that outpaced most military timetables, the man still retained his rugged good looks, especially in his new blue and gray uniform jacket, and the navy trousers with a golden yellow stripe down the leg. She smiled, taking her coffee to the table and settling down across from Jack as he took a bite from the oatmeal biscuit.

"Sleep okay?" she asked.

"And how," he answered. "Like a really sleepy rock."

Jack smiled, meeting Doc's eyes across the sunbathed table. He'd been feeling an ever-growing sense of impending calamity since the close call at Oba's fort, but hadn't figured out how best to broach the subject. Still, her soft gaze filled him with a warmth and security he'd never known. In his youth, he'd worn bravado as his armor. After the war, he'd replaced it with professional competence. And now, peering into this frightening abyss, he didn't even feel he could rely on that. But Doc made it seem unnecessary. Jack felt as long as they had each other's six, there was nothing to fear. He wished he could put that concept into words, but he was painfully gun-shy when it came being vulnerable with Doc. She'd already broken his heart once. He'd gladly work alongside her if it meant soaking up all that was good about her company, but he wasn't ready to offer up his heart as sacrifice —not again.

Doc shifted in her seat and cleared her throat, and Jack thought for sure that she'd been reading his mind.

"I've been thinking... about Paris," she offered, a melancholy look falling across her face.

Jack instinctively reached across the table to take her hand in his. "You okay, Doc?"

She blinked away some tears and returned to meet his gaze.

"It was more than a good time, wasn't it?" she asked.

Jack's face became a comic mask. "Sure!" he said. "It was great! Why? What are you getting at?"

Doc looked away, then back at him. "I want you to know that turning you down was not an easy decision to make."

His forehead furrowed. "Fair enough," he assured her. "I completely understand. We had different lives…"

"It's just that…" Doc began, trying desperately to find the words. "You remember I was telling you about—"

Suddenly Rivets burst in on the ship's speakers. "Crossing the border into Brazil, Cap. Might wanna come up and check our course. And Duke's got news from HQ."

Jack squeezed her hand. "Hang onto that thought," he smiled. "We'll come back to it."

Doc returned a wistful version of his smile and nodded, letting him slip away onto the bridge.

The sprawling green canopy of the Amazon jungle bore no physical indicator of an international border. They knew their location due to copious charts and a superb compass.

"Morning, fellas." Jack said as he tagged Rivets out and slipped into the pilot's chair, switching off engines and non-essential systems.

The mechanic trudged aft to his quarters. "Battery array's fully charged, Cap," he said. "You should be A-OK."

Jack nodded. "Duke, what's the news on the wireless?"

"Unfortunately," Duke nodded, "we just received word that our contact Mr. Salyer was assaulted in Port au Prince just after you left the office."

"Oh no," Jack gasped. "And the Cross?"

"It's gone missing," said Duke.

Jack's brow wrinkled into a troubled road map. "All right," He said finally. "Let's get a radio reading."

"Aye, Captain."

Doc entered and took her seat at the nav station as Duke powered up the radio detector, sending out the familiar *deet-deet-deet-deet* in ever widening waves.

"Nothing, sir," Duke announced, disappointed. "At least nothing of *Luftpanzer* scale." Then he paused, squinting at the amber glass screen. "Hang on. Picking up several small aircraft about fifty miles south-southwest of our position."

The first impact shook the *Daedalus* from stem to stern, rattling the crew. Duke threw Jack a concerned look. "What the devil—??"

"The heck was that?" Jack worried aloud.

Doc strained to look out the side starboard bridge windows. "Something hit us!" she exclaimed.

Jack leaned back to look at Duke. "I didn't hear shooting—that had to have been ground fire. Anti-aircraft!"

Rivets reappeared at the bridge hatch, red-faced and wide-eyed. "Oh, I'm not a happy man!"

A second impact rocked the bridge, and it took a moment for everyone to regain their bearings.

"Duke," Jack urged. "Can you get a read on where these are coming from?"

Duke shook his head. "Negative. Signal can't penetrate the forest."

Jack hit the *TALK* button on his console. "Deadeye?" he called. "Whatcha got topside?"

The gunner's voice crackled back in his ear. "Uh, Cap?" Deadeye said. "I'm not sure how to explain this..."

The call was interrupted by the staccato bass drum of the Hotchkiss. He was shooting at something, but there were no flying targets around, no incoming gunfire.

"Explain what, Charlie?"

Then Deadeye was back on the radio, and the urgency in his voice was something Jack hadn't heard since Italy. "You might want to power up the engines and climb."

The Hotchkiss stuttered again, and a third impact shook the *Daedalus*.

As Doc steadied herself on the console, she caught a glimpse of something zoom past the ship, careening off in a spiral trajectory over the jungle. *Impossible,* she thought. *It couldn't be.*

"That couldn't be what it looked like," she offered.

Jack did his best to peer out from the bridge windows, but he'd obviously missed that last one. "What did it look like?"

Doc lowered her tone. "Like a man, strapped to a rocket."

Jack threw a bewildered glance over his shoulder in Doc's direction.

"There goes another!" Duke pointed.

The strange shape of a human being tied to a four-foot-long incendiary rocket whistled past them into the sky, arcing down and disappearing into the green.

Jack and Doc both saw it that time. And they both noticed something peculiar about this projectile. The human portion was skeletal, desiccated, dressed in haphazard rags.

"Except it wasn't a man," Jack said.

Doc finished his thought. "It looked like a dead body."

Another impact shook the bridge.

Rivets could no longer contain his shock, anger and disbelief. All three manifested aloud. "Who in the living blazes is shootin' dead bodies at us??"

"I think we know who," Jack stated. He was quickly back to business, which was another thing Doc loved about him. "Duke, cut the detector. Firing up the engines. Full power, maximum lift."

Engines spun up in their electric whine, the twin thrust pods tilted to a 90 degree angle, and the *Daedalus* rose vertically into the air.

"I don't know what Crowley is pulling," said Jack, "but I'm not sticking around to find out."

Doc stepped forward to lean in over the back of the pilot's chair. "Jack," she said quietly. "It could have just been the wind, but it really looked like the last one... well, his limbs were moving."

Jack swallowed and pretended not to hear her. The thought was too horrible and strange for this early in the morning, and he'd only just had breakfast.

Still the strange projectiles came, one in three making impact with the hull, the rest disappearing into the rainforest. Eventually the *Daedalus* pulled up out of range.

Deadeye's voice crackled over the comms. "Cap? I could use some help up here. And if Doc could come too..."

Jack and Doc exchanged a brief look, then Jack was unstrapping from the chair, hitting the *TALK* button. "On our way," he answered. "Duke, you're on the stick. Rivets, I want you in the engine room to make absolutely sure those batteries stay full and the props keep spinning."

Rivets disappeared toward the engine room, Duke took over at the pilot's console, and Jack and Doc went to the ladder just aft of the bridge hatch. Doc paused a moment, remembering something.

"You go on up," she said. "I'm right behind you."

Doc turned to the locker directly opposite the ladder and opened it. The strange looking weapon Deadeye had been playing with at the docks in Port au Prince stood inside. She grabbed the Tesla gun and slung it over her shoulder, returning to the ladder and climbing for the roof hatch.

# # #

Jack unlatched the top hatch and swung it open. Although in the tropics, the wind at 10,000 feet was cold as it whipped across his face and down the airship's dorsal envelope. He quickly lowered the goggles from his leather flight helmet, staggering for balance as he made his way to Deadeye at the gun emplacement.

Doc was right behind him, her boots finding purchase on the other side of the guns.

Jack clapped Deadeye on the shoulder to get his attention. The marksman turned goggled eyes to look at his captain.

"Whatcha got, Charlie?" Jack yelled above the whistling wind.

"Dunno, Cap!" Deadeye answered. "Looks like those *zombis* we saw in Haiti, but a lot more dead!"

Doc looked downrange from the Hotchkiss guns and saw a shape moving up the spine of the ship.

"Problem is," Deadeye explained, "they're not!"

Suddenly the shape was coming at them like a savage lioness, growling and screeching, foamy spittle dripping from its dead mouth. It scanned them with milky yellow eyes that peered out of deep sockets, leathery flesh tearing away in small chunks by the wind. Its fingernails were long and sharp, its skin tone a pale, sickly gray-green. And strapped to its back was the rocket that had brought it there, now just dead weight.

Doc pointed out the rapidly approaching ghoul, and Jack nodded. She unslung the electric carbine from her shoulder and powered on the main switch. The hum of the rifle's power cell was inaudible over the steady white noise of the wind, but the light display told her the device was ready. She aimed the gun at the creature and pulled the trigger. A brilliant blast of blue-white lightning erupted from the metallic ball at the end of the barrel, tearing the ghoul into three equally-portioned, writhing masses, each of which flew off into the airship's wake.

Deadeye gave a thumbs up to Doc, who signaled Jack to turn around.

Another ghoul had made impact with the side of the *Daedalus*, and had clawed its way onto the spine. Jack spun around, drawing both pistols and emptying three shots apiece into the thing, which was enough to dislodge it and send it spinning away to the forest below.

Deadeye pointed behind Doc, who turned to see another ghoul shambling toward the three of them. The Tesla carbine sparked again, sending a tendril of lightning to its target, ripping the ghoul apart.

"These aren't *Vodou zombis*, Jack!" Doc yelled over the wind. "These are some kind of resurrected dead!"

Jack wasn't sure of the full implications of what she said, but he nodded anyway. This was her wheelhouse. He noticed Deadeye swinging the guns toward another ghoul scrambling up the spine near the rear port stabilizer, and flagged him to wait.

"Don't waste the incendiaries!" Jack shouted. "I've got it!"

He waited until the creature had cleared half the distance between them, gave it three bullets from each pistol and watched it fall to the canvas. It slid down the curvature of the airship's envelope and was flung away by the wind.

"I don't see any more, Cap!" Deadeye announced, looking around them.

"They don't seem so tough, but I wouldn't want to let them inside. We need to find someplace to tie up and make a hull inspection!" Jack hollered through the biting air current.

Then Deadeye saw it. Perhaps three miles distant, spread across the tree canopy, lay a huge structure.

Jack noticed Deadeye's gaze and looked himself. His eyes wide with surprise, he flagged Doc to have a look.

Doc turned, agape at the sheer scale of the structure. "It... It looks like a city—built in the tree canopy!"

- Chapter 14 -

The ancient carved stone head of a forgotten deity gazed out from the side of the temple. Though the carving resembled the Olmec art of Mexico and Guatemala, the influence of Olmec culture had never touched the ancient people of the Brazilian rainforest. This was a wholly different and distinct culture, a predecessor of the local Kuikuro people. Once cleared and open to the sun above, the complex was now covered in vines and jungle greenery reclaiming its former possessions. It was perhaps not the largest of ancient temple pyramids, but it was among the oldest and most complete in the region. A stairway of white stone led from the jungle floor to an altar and ceremonial brazier at the top. Like most pre-Columbian Mesoamerican cultures, these people had practiced ritual bloodletting, so the front stairs were bisected by a carved gutter, stained a rust red over eons of use. Several smaller constructions littered the landscape, looking like stone-capped root cellars. A team of Silver Star archaeologists had already determined them to be crypts made for royalty, and had carefully but thoroughly pillaged them of anything valuable.

A small army of Amazon natives wandered to and fro, hacking away at the jungle, clearing stones and rubble, or carrying baskets of debris to the midden heap outside the camp. They were overseen by Silver Star commandos in gray fatigues and MP-18s, who watched them with suspicious eyes. Natives who were too sick or weak to work were locked in a gated pen in the center of the camp, awaiting the pleasure of Aleister Crowley.

The clearing around the temple pyramid was a good 200 yards in each direction, though to the west most of that was taken up by a small lake. And floating atop the lake was the mammoth zeppelin *Luftpanzer*, surrounded by a few Caspar U.1 seaplanes, all painted in Silver Star colors. A rudimentary pier ran from the camp to the planes and giant dirigible, the opposite side of the camp filled with stained canvas Army tents for the fifty or so Silver Star operatives at work here.

Captain Ecke found Maria sitting on the lower temple stairs, gazing at the sky through a pair of field glasses. He'd been watching her "rocket zombies" with his own spyglass, and couldn't help but be impressed.

"Maria," he began, not knowing quite what to say. "Your ploy succeeded! The *Daedalus* has passed over our position."

She smiled, lowering the binoculars to hang around her neck. "Of course, *mein Kapitain.*"

Ecke was becoming animated. "And missiles of the living dead... what horrible genius!"

"Indeed," Maria nodded. "When manpower is needed, what better source than the dead? They do not require food or pay. They are in every way expendable."

A commando strode with purpose to the base of the stairs and saluted the two officers. "*Meine Führerin!* Herr Crowley awaits you in his quarters!"

"Well Captain Ecke," said Maria as she stood, ignoring the saluting soldier. "It seems the time has come. The ritual is almost upon us." And with that, she followed the commando across the compound, leaving Ecke alone on the temple stairs.

# # #

Rivets passed along the central powerplant of the *Daedalus*, monitoring the eight DiMarco-Edison Mk3 reactionless gyroscopes in sequence. Each generator provided 100 kilowatts of power to the ship's systems, including the giant turbofans in the outboard thrust engines. The battery array and alternators were split on either side of the entry hatch, with gauges and monitors that displayed power generation, consumption, and various other metrics that engineers liked to keep track of.

Sleep-deprived and grouchy, Rivets tried to shake the image of an animated corpse strapped to a rocket. But to no avail. There was a crash of broken glass and he turned toward the starboard window panels to see that the aftermost pane had been shattered, and a living ghoul now clawed its way into the engine room from the outside hull. Rivets had to blink to make sure the thing in front of him, bent under the weight of the primitive rocket, was real and not an artifact of this morning's ordeal.

"What the heck??" Rivets exclaimed. "What gives??"

The moment it snarled at him, swiping bony claws at his face, he knew it was real. And it scared him to death.

"No!" he warned, backing away toward the closed hatchway. "Stay back!"

The hideous ghoul snarled an animal growl and bared skeletal teeth.

Suddenly Rivets remembered the large spanner he used to tighten or loosen the bolts on the battery contacts. He reached for his back pocket and produced a foot-long crescent wrench of galvanized steel, top-heavy like a medieval mace.

"Ya see this wrench, pal?" Rivets taunted. "I'm not afraid to use it!"

He swung the improvised weapon at the snarling invader, cracking a dent in the thin metal body of the rocket on its back. Clear liquid began to leak, and Rivets could smell aviation fuel. Then the creature struck with a clawed hand, knocking the wrench away. It hit hard against the battery array, which erupted in a fountain of sparks and tendrils of electricity. One such tendril traveled up the leg of the ghoul to the rocket body and the leaking fuel.

Rivets dove for the deck just as the rocket's reserve tank exploded. The concussion knocked the air from his lungs as the engine room was plastered with ancient human remains and tiny shards of metal. The last thing he saw was the gaping hole in the gondola, smoke billowing out over the green canopy below. The ship listed over, and he realized he'd lost his grip on the engine platform.

Then he was falling, and everything went dark.

# # #

Jack and Doc were near the bottom of the ladder to the bridge hatch when the *Daedalus* shook violently and leaned over. Jack let go and jumped the last few feet to the deck, guiding Doc the rest of the way.

They burst onto the bridge to see Duke fighting a losing battle with the ship's controls.

"Duke," said Jack, "What was that explosion?"

"Strap in or hang onto something, sir!" Duke snapped. "We're going down!"

Jack and Doc saw the jungle canopy looming up from below and their eyes went wide.

Doc flung herself into the nav station chair, and Jack braced himself in the hatchway.

"Hang on!" Duke warned.

The *Daedalus* came in low over the treetops, and the starboard engine nacelle finally snagged on the upthrust limb of a 200-foot-tall ceiba tree. The anchor effect whipped the airship around backward, scattering loose supplies and breaking several of the starboard window panels in the gondola. The ship came to rest on the flattened jungle canopy, its tail end sunk into the trees, nose angled up as if it were a person trying desperately not to drown.

The bridge sat at an angle, Duke no longer able to see the trees below.

Jack waited for the ship to settle further, but nothing happened. "Seems we've arrived at our destination," he said.

Duke unstrapped the pilot harness and

tried to find some footing at the odd angle. "Any landing you can walk away from, eh wot?"

Jack moved toward the nav station to help Doc stand. "Hear, hear, Duke," he replied. "Well said, indeed."

"I wonder what happened," Doc puzzled.

Jack stepped over to the radio console and saw that auxiliary power was still functional. He hit the *TALK* button.

"Deadeye," he called. "You okay?"

There was an uncomfortable silence before Deadeye's voice crackled over the bridge loud-speaker. "A-OK, Cap," he said. "Pretty smooth, as crashes go."

Jack smiled the gallows humor smile of the World War veteran. "Alright, you stay put and keep an eye on things topside. Stand by." He paused momentarily, then called back to the engine room. "Rivets, you there, pal?"

Static was the only response.

"The explosion could have knocked out his intercom," Doc noted.

Jack took his finger off the console and waved the other two to follow him. "Let's get aft and check on Rivets. We can make a dam-age assessment from there."

He exited the bridge and disappeared down the angled gantry, Doc close on his heels.

"Right-o," Duke acknowledged, following

Doc through the hatch.

The main gondola lights were flickering, but the red emergency lamps shone steady in the dim light. Jack was the first to arrive at the engine room hatch. Turning the locking lever counter-clockwise, he pulled the hatch open and entered the engine compartment. "Hey, Rivets?" he called out, but no one answered.

Light poured into the engine room from the giant hole in the gondola wall. The surfaces of the gauges and readouts were blackened with soot, and some of the more delicate components had melted into slag. Six of the eight glass casings for the gyroscopes were cracked or shattered, and all but two had stopped functioning.

"Oh dear," Duke said as he entered the room. "What a mess."

Duke saw the two spinning gyroscopes and went to shut them off. "We should shut down the main battery array," he said.

Jack nodded and went to the console on the left side of the hatch. He noticed the wrench, now blackened and burned, was wedged between the contacts of three batteries. He indicated for Doc to go to the right console. Wiping away some of the soot on the glass gauges, he managed to find a main power shutoff and pulled the handle to the *OFF* position. Doc followed his lead. The cabin lights ceased flickering and went dark. The remaining gyroscopes wound down. The ship swayed gently with the movement of the trees in the wind, and they found it eerily quiet.

"I say," Duke remarked. "Where's Rivets?"

Jack nodded at the gaping hole in the ship. "Only one way he could have gone."

Doc didn't want to imagine that scenario. "Oh, you don't think—"

"Let's find out," Jack said grimly. "Through this new door."

They climbed down through the hole to find a network of sturdy limbs and branches intertwined with each other, so thick as to be walkable. They hailed Deadeye from below, and the sharpshooter scrambled down the guide wires to join them in the search. Jack led the way, calling for Rivets.

"Can you see him anywhere?" Doc asked.

Jack shook his head, squinting against the bright sunlight. "Branches are too thick to see much. Let's keep going."

The heat was oppressive, and soon the four had shed their new uniforms, pressing on in boots, trousers, and undershirts. They made their way some 200 yards from the ship when Deadeye noticed movement in the trees ahead. He tapped Jack on the shoulder and pointed.

"What the devil is that?" Jack asked.

The sound of tribal drums erupted from

the jungle around them, and it suddenly looked like the canopy was alive with natives, scurrying and scampering through the trees the way a small monkey would. They were everywhere—painted, pierced, adorned with feathers and bones, and armed with long wooden lances and hunting bows.

"Keep an eye on those weapons," Jack warned. "A lot of the Amazon tribes tip their points with poison."

"They're coming closer," Deadeye warned.

Jack slipped a pistol out of its holster. "Fire a couple warning shots with me, Charlie. Maybe that will scare them off."

Jack and Deadeye squeezed off two rounds apiece, firing into the air. It had no appreciable effect on the circling natives. Jack fired a third shot, clipping a high branch above the hunters. Still nothing.

Suddenly a jungle vine flew out of the canopy and lassoed around Jack's shoulders. Before he could call out in surprise, a second, third and fourth vine had entangled the other crewmembers. Doc lost her balance and fell to her side. Deadeye levered his Winchester under the vine lasso binding his upper body. Jack heard it and warned him off.

"Deadeye, no!" Jack cried. "All of you, try not to struggle! They obviously want us alive, or they could have shot us with those hunting bows!"

Each of the *Daedalus* crew knew they were taking a huge risk. If felt unnatural to let themselves be abducted without fighting back. But Jack McGraw's best survival skill was his instinct, and they trusted that.

The natives crowded in, binding all four by the hands and feet, securing them to long horizontal poles for transport. Doc looked at Jack as they were hoisted between the brawny shoulders of several natives.

"What you think, Jack?" she asked.

Jack wished he could scratch the itch caused by the drying rivulet of sweat across his ear. "I think they likely know where Rivets is," he said. "And if we mind our manners, they might take us to him."

Then Jack and the crew were whisked away through the jungle trees.

- Chapter 15 -

Maria ducked under the canvas flap and entered the field tent of her master, the infamous mage Aleister Crowley. His back faced the door, but even so, she could see the leather belt cinched around his left arm, the wooden desk in front of him strewn with heroin paraphernalia. He'd heard her coming well before she'd approached the tent, and exhibited no shame in being discovered like this.

"Ah. Maria," he greeted, remaining with his back to her.

The glint of an antique gold cross inset with gems reached her eyes from the corner of the tent, only partially unwrapped from its canvas and brown paper shroud. At least the agents Crowley had sent to steal the Cross of Cadiz had been effective.

She heard the clatter of the syringe on the metal tray, and he turned to face her as the chemical rush washed over him. He staggered momentarily, and she rushed to his side, helping him sit as he stumbled toward his cot.

"How progresses your campaign against

that gang of villains Edison has set upon me?" Crowley asked in a surprisingly thin voice for such a sturdy fellow. He spoke in well-educated King's English, similar to Duke's posh accent.

An otherwise vital man of 50, Crowley's body had been ravaged by a constant barrage of venereal disease, heroin and cocaine addiction. Standing a respectable 5'10", he was nonetheless carrying an extra 40 pounds of weight, and his shaved head revealed a pair of intense, deep-set brown eyes which rested atop dark, fleshy bags. It was a body that had been in peak shape in its youth, but with age there had come the tendency to forgo sport and physical activity in exchange for pleasures of the flesh and broadening of the mind—and with it, ever-increasing mystical power.

Maria knew him to be the most powerful living wizard, despite his current state of endorphin haze from the *piqure* he'd just administered to himself. It was not his somewhat compromised physicality, however, which was the source of his allure with both males and females; but the radiant charisma and power that emanated from his soul. Maria had been lured to his bed more than once by that radiance. Crowley was famous for his practice of sexual magicks, and she had been a willing participant for the past seven years. She and her master knew each other's body, mind, and spirit with a casual familiarity. There was an implied trust between them that precious few of The Great Beast's acolytes enjoyed.

"We forced the *Daedalus* to crash in the canopy about ten miles away. There is no update on the crew, but my forward observers have reported much activity among the Tree People in the area." Maria knelt at his side and gently tended him, loosening the cinch and pulling it from his arm. She noted the track marks down his bare arm, and how the most recent injection site was oozing blood. She pulled a handkerchief from the desk and dabbed at the wound.

Crowley closed his eyes and surrendered to Maria's care. "Excellent," he said. "And Jack McGraw still has no idea who you are?"

Maria paused and closed her eyes, remembering a time of great promise and terrible tragedy.

# # #

France, May, 1918

The young barmaid was a comely Swiss girl by the name of Eva Freitag. She'd only been in Beauvois for a month, but she was already a popular attraction among the Allied officers who frequented the La Chance tavern. Statuesque, raven-haired and of pale complexion, she was often called "Snow White" by the British soldiers who passed through. She'd developed a reputation for being generous with her pulls from the tap and enthusiasm between the sheets, a combination which won her many fans among the British and French Armies as well as her real employer, the Head of Austro-Hungarian military intelligence, General Arthur Giesl von Gieslingen. In fact her name was not Eva, and she wasn't Swiss. She was Maria Gunnhild, a proud and patriotic German spy for the Central Powers. She was fluent in English and French, had studied the principles of Tantra, and she was game to do anything for the war effort.

An exhausted Allied officer with a few drinks in his belly was willing to spill a lot of interesting military information during post-coital pillow talk, and "Eva" was very good at information extraction. She also had a talent for compartmentalizing morality, for while she trysted for the Central Powers, she was also engaged to a famous German ace: Hans Heinrich. He was a dashing Bavarian with a promising future and a Heidelberg scar that made women swoon. Best of all, he was ambitious and charismatic, and Maria Gunnhild could not wait to become Frau Heinrich.

She remembered their last meeting in Köln, their last lovemaking, their last embrace at the train station as he shipped back to the

front lines. With the promise of a Central Powers victory and a marriage to her true love,
"Eva" was assigned to Beauvois. She served
beer and wine with a friendly smile and negotiated for "after hours" services with the con-
sent of the proprietor, a silver-haired
grandfather who looked the other way on such
matters. After all, what business was it of his
if the girl needed some extra money to send
home to her family? Besides, he made an extra ten percent on her room.

The month had gone like clockwork. The
only officer in the area she hadn't been able to
get into bed was a pilot, Captain McGraw with
the 32nd Squadron. He tended to arrive with a
comrade or two, knock back a couple of
rounds, maybe sing a song, and then disappear for other venues and diversions. It was a
shame, really—she found him quite attractive.

Until that day.

On that day, he became the object of her
hate.

She was serving a table of French soldiers,
playfully slapping the Lieutenant who was getting handsy with her, when McGraw strutted
in, flush from victory, the smell of engine oil
and smoke still lingering on his flight leathers.
He was with two mates: a stocky fellow they
called Rivets, and a British munitions officer
by the last name of Willis (but everyone called
him Duke). They pushed the grinning pilot to

the bar, demanded a round of beer, and proceeded to toast the room on behalf of "Captain Stratosphere".

The man who had just shot down that German devil, Hans Heinrich.

Eva's tray dropped to the floor, shattered glass flying everywhere. The soldiers around her did their best to help her clean up the mess, but she just focused on the three men at the bar. Reveling in the death of her betrothed. Her true love.

She watched them laugh, and drink, and laugh some more. She watched McGraw relate the story to another group of pilots, even pantomiming the aerial tactics with his hands. He was pleased with himself, wasn't he?

That night, she packed up her few belongings and left Beauvois, never to return. Never to feel joy again. Never to love again. In its place grew a black hatred of Captain McGraw, and by extension everyone and everything he loved.

And she swore she'd destroy it all.

# # #

Crowley's eyes were closed and he imagined the scene Maria described.

"And when your friend, 'Captain Stratosphere', shot your betrothed down, you pledged your vengeance upon him..." he mumbled the end of a story he never grew tired of hearing.

"Yes," Maria nodded, lifting a canteen of water to Crowley's lips to let him drink. "I hated him as my enemy in war, and I hated him as my enemy in life. I pledge death to Captain Stratosphere, and to those he loves."

"Very well, Maria," Crowley said softly. "Very well."

Previously serene, he suddenly opened his eyes and gazed at Maria intently. "You realize the importance of the summoning ritual tonight? Is the temple made ready? Are the sacrifices plentiful?"

"Yes," she answered, bowing her head.

"For we summon Choronzon," Crowley explained, "Dweller in the Abyss. He commands a demonic legion which in turn will be mine to command, as I will control Choronzon. No nation will dare stand against the Silver Star. This summoning will allow us to work our will upon the world."

She knew her master was fully in the "dragon's embrace" now, rambling plots of which she was well aware, as he leaned to one side and began to slur his words.

"You serve me well," he said. "And once we have completed the ceremony tonight, I will set you free to finish your vendetta against Captain McGraw."

Maria guided her mentor in the occult to a resting position with his head on a pillow, gently caressing his bald head as he drifted deeper into his heroin haze.

"Thank you, my master."

# # #

The arboreal natives were swift and sure-footed through the tangled causeways of the tree canopy, as if the knowledge of every dip and rise, pit and crevasse were inborn. With two hunters at the front of each pole, and two at the rear, the Daedalus crew were carried quickly through the thick branches and leaves. Before long, the tangled vines and branches had become carved wooden planks assembled into paths which led into a magnificent wooden city.

The throb of ceremonial drums echoed through the jungle treetops, and painted natives in simple skins, faces pierced with barbs of bone and wood scurried to and fro in preparation. For what, Doc hadn't a clue.

Single homes of rattan with thatched roofs stood proudly at the outer perimeter of local political power, concentrating inward in circles —like the growth rings of a tree—and culminating at the city center. The seat of power was the central hall, a round structure easily

100 feet across and roofed like the other dwellings, with an open chimney for the community fire and braced by enormous rattan columns which had been ornately carved with sacred tribal designs. There were no walls as such; the structure was open to the air on all sides between the columns.

The crew were brought into the central hall, and were grateful for the cooler shade. For a moment Jack felt a pang of fear that this had been a bad idea. There was already a fire crackling in the giant ceramic brazier in the middle. It was large enough to accommodate the carrying poles two at a time. He had no desire to end up the main course at a cannibal feast. Then he reminded himself to be more generous—after all, the natives had gone out of their way *not* to kill them thus far.

Across the hall on a raised dais sat an ornate wooden throne, upon which sat a stunningly beautiful native woman of mature age. She was dressed in jaguar skins trimmed with silver, her ebony hair plaited and adorned with the feathers of colorful tropical birds. Armlets of silver and gold sparkled in the firelight, contrasting against her deep tan complexion. She stood, and as she raised her hand, the drumming ceased.

"*Atok! Arrendi mah-kor!*" she commanded, and suddenly the crew found their bonds cut with sharpened stone knives. They were ushered around the fire to the wooden steps rising to the throne. Strong hands pushed them to their knees, then the native hunters retreated to either side of the steps. Jack realized the psychological effect of placing them on their knees at the bottom of the steps, with a large fire behind them and armed warriors to either side. It gave the woman on the throne a much more diplomatically desirable quality. *Why yes, we'd much rather deal with you than the warriors, the fire, or the jungle below.*

The woman began to descend the timber stairs. Her feet were bare, like the rest of the natives, but adorned with silver anklets and rings of boar tusk matching those on her arms. She carried a spear that Doc presumed more ceremonial than functional—a rattan shaft wrapped in leather strips, adorned with feathers and tipped in a 14-inch long translucent blade of hand-chipped red quartz. When she arrived at the lowest step, she looked at Jack and his crew with narrow eyes.

"Who are you, strangers?" she said in a low, soft voice.

Jack blinked. He hadn't expected English. No one had.

"You speak English?" Jack stammered.

"I speak English," she replied. "We have traded with Yankee priests. You are Yankees, no?"

Doc assumed by "Yankee priests" she meant American missionaries. Such interactions must have taken place on the jungle floor, or word would have spread of this magnificent wooden city in the treetops.

Jack nodded, introducing his crew. "American and British. I'm Jack McGraw, captain of the airship *Daedalus*. This is Dorothy Starr, Charlie Dalton and Edward Willis."

The woman straightened, standing tall over the kneeling crew. She planted the butt of the spear firmly on the lower step. "I am Alanna, queen of the Tree People."

Doc knew a bit about native cultures of the Amazon region, and this revelation followed the norm. Many tribal names translated into English as the dominant quality of the tribe. The Fierce People. The Invisible People. The River People. The only thing that wasn't "normal" was their home environment and slightly higher technology level, judging from the construction of the place.

"And you live here, in the jungle canopy?" Doc asked.

"Yes," Alanna answered. "This is my kingdom among the trees. We lived peacefully here, until you sky-people came..."

Jack slowly rose to one knee. "Most gracious Alanna," he offered. "We're looking for a giant airship—many times bigger than the one we came in."

"But you are not like the others," she interrupted, taking measure of the crew as she paced around and in front of them.

"Others?" Doc wondered aloud.

Alanna fixed Doc with a suspicious gaze. "The others who came from the sky, with their guns and evil magic."

Duke leaned over to Jack, muttering, "That sounds like a perfect description of the Silver Star."

Deadeye overheard the comment. "Sure does," he agreed.

"Yes!" Alanna snapped, pointing the translucent red spear point at Duke, much to his surprise and dismay. "They wear a silver star, and follow a man called Cro-lee."

"Crowley!" Doc exclaimed.

Then the spear was inches from Doc's throat and Alanna circled her like a jungle cat.

"What do you know of this man?" she demanded.

Jack tried as best he could to bring the native queen's focus back on himself, for better or worse.

"Is he here? In the Amazon?" he asked earnestly.

Alanna turned her attention back to the captain, and Doc sighed in relief.

"His camp is below the Temple of the Elders," Alanna said. "He has hostages he means to sacrifice in a dark ritual. Some of my people are among them. We have tried to send warriors to bring them back, but the evil sky-people guns are too strong. They kill without thought."

"I say," whispered Duke, "this sounds like a golden opportunity, Jack."

Doc regarded Alanna plaintively. "What about Rivets?"

Jack clarified, "One of my crew went missing in the crash. Have your people seen him?"

Alanna regarded Jack. He could tell she was softening to their presence. All he needed was an opening to propose an alliance.

"Was he a short, angry man with whiskers like a capybara?" she asked.

"I don't know what that is," Jack said, "but it sure sounds like Rivets."

Alanna's tone darkened. "He was taken by the gray suits of the Silver Star," she said. "They are to sacrifice him... with many of my people."

"Oh no," Doc gasped.

Duke frowned. "Heavens."

Jack spread his arms in a gesture of openness, palms upward. "Alanna," he said softly. "Can your scouts guide us to this... Temple of the Elders? To Crowley's camp?"

The Amazon queen stared at Jack, weighing every possible option and outcome.

Finally, Jack added, "We'll try to rescue your people as well as our friend—and stop whatever evil plan Crowley is up to."

Suddenly the spear point was at his neck and he felt it lift his chin. He accepted her invitation to stand. Then the spear was at her side and she looked hard into his eyes.

"You are a very different sky-man, Jack Mah-grah," Alanna said.

She turned on her heel and ascended back up the stairs to her throne on the dais. Taking her seat, she nodded at the group. "We will help you," she said. "If you swear to release my people."

Jack bowed his head respectfully. "We'll do our best, your majesty."

- Chapter 16 -

The crew were ushered to an open-air assembly area, and all four immediately began to sweat again. Sunlight blazed down over the green blanket of the jungle canopy, bathing the tree city in a saturated white haze. Native warriors, both male and female, armed with spears, bows and javelin-like hunting arrows began to congregate around them. Some took an interest in Deadeye's features, which were similar to their own. They delighted when he spoke to them in Cherokee, although they couldn't understand a word. One slender scout took Duke's cap and put it on, mugging for the audience. There was a burst of communal laughter, which increased when the scout put the hat onto a young girl.

Doc squinted through the harsh light at Jack, who appeared distracted. She thought she knew why.

"That Alanna is quite a woman," she said innocently.

"Sure," said Jack. "If you like that sort of thing." Then he added, almost under his breath, "She's no Doc Starr," and wandered toward a group of warriors near one of the wooden gantries leading out of the city.

Doc's heart swelled. "Good answer," she smiled.

The group was introduced to one of Queen Alanna's personal guards, Katoc, a tall man with bronze skin and a face painted clay red from the nose to the shaved crest of his proud skull. As a revered warrior among the Tree People with some command of English, Katoc had been assigned to lead the Sky People through the jungle to the Temple of the Elders, and aid them in liberating the native hostages there.

"If you trick us or fail to free our people," Katoc threatened, "we will leave you in the jungle to die."

Jack knew the importance of honor among elder civilizations; it was a quality the imperialist cultures of Europe and America had largely lost contact with. He clapped a hand on Katoc's shoulder.

"We will not trick you," he promised. "We wish only peace and friendship with your people." He turned to address the crowd. Those who comprehended English translated haphazardly for those who didn't. "But we face a uniquely evil enemy. One who kills without conscience. One who distorts the world with dark magics. One who would enslave not just your people, but all of the tribes of the Amazon."

Jack paced in a circle, looking into the eyes of every native man, woman and child. "We must show this enemy no fear, and we must not rest until we have saved your people and driven every last one of the Silver Star from your jungle."

Jack glanced at the great hall where Alanna was emerging into the noonday sun.

"Or killed them," he added.

A murmur of approval and primal aggression swept through the crowd.

Jack turned back to Katoc, fixing him in a solemn stare. "Katoc, we swear to fight side by side with the Tree People, unto victory... or death."

If Katoc had any prior reservations about the motives of the Sky People, he shunted them from his mind. At least for now, and the foreseeable future, they would be his brethren in battle. He responded with his own hand on Jack's shoulder.

"We will fight... or die... together," he said.

A cheer went up from the crowd, and Jack smiled at his crew. "Ammo check!" he ordered.

Doc had never seen him so completely in command, and not in some blustery, macho, military way. This was a man invested in the safety of his crew, pledging his life in the service of others. She tried to present a front of all-business, but even in the simple act of checking the cylinder of her revolver, she felt an almost adolescent giddiness—feelings she hadn't felt since Paris.

A group of native scouts escorted Jack and the crew to the wrecked *Daedalus*, where they stocked up on ammunition and a few necessities. Doc took the opportunity to slip into a fresh shirt, which she tied above the navel. It would have been a daring fashion choice back home in New Jersey, but here in the jungle— among nearly-naked warriors—function won out over propriety. She stocked every loop in her gun belt with a fresh cartridge, looking very much like a western silent movie star. The lodestone was tucked into her right front trouser pocket, just in case. She realized the risk of taking it into a Silver Star camp where she could easily be killed or captured, in which case it would become the property of an enemy who would abuse its power. But it might also be a useful weapon in their fight. So along it came.

Deadeye asked Jack his preference for weaponry: the Winchester carbine or the Springfield. Jack told him they needed every person on the ground in this operation, thus the only sniper cover would be a small unit of natives. Deadeye loaded the Winchester full and stuffed a box of .45 long Colt rounds into his ammo pack.

Duke grabbed a canvas satchel full of the strange new grenades they'd been given in Port au Prince, and took some extra ammo for his Webbley service revolver.

Jack reloaded his pistol magazines and added a couple of spare clips each to the pouches on his belt. He kept his trench knife and a small pair of binoculars, and tied a cotton bandanna around his neck to absorb the sweat running down from his head.

Then they were back on the maze of thick limbs and branches that made up the elevated highway through the jungle trees. Doc was envious of the barefoot natives who were able to take the path at a brisk jog, rather than carefully tread each step worrying about a twelve-story fall to the rainforest floor. For the *Daedalus* crew, it was slow going. Traversing miles of the crisscrossed limbs of giant rattan, lapuna and rubber trees, scampering down vines and ducking under mossy overhangs, the crew was a ragged, sweaty mess. Deadeye recalled his Army basic training at Wilmington, but not even North Carolina was this hot and humid.

After about five miles travel above the jungle floor, the trail linked up with a network of deer paths on the ground, and the group was able to move much faster. Finally, the sun dipped in the western sky and the mosquitoes came out in swarms. Katoc showed the Sky People how to crush leaves of the *Citronella mucronata* into an oily balm that would keep the insectoid vampires at bay.

They continued over a small creek and up a trail thick with beautiful, toxic plants. The trail forked at a 45-degree angle, and Katoc sent three scouts to northward. Then he led everyone else on the easterly trail, which curved through a half-mile of dense foliage. The path ended at a cluster of massive wimba trees and strangler figs clinging to a rocky hillside which overlooked the Temple of the Elders. The vine tendrils wove a perfect screen to hide behind, allowing the party to watch the goings-on within the camp with impunity, almost a natural hunting blind. Katoc shimmied up a natural ladder of vines and footholds in a massive tree trunk to keep watch above, while the *Daedalus* crew found themselves collapsing in a larger hollow. The rest of the natives were so adept at stealth and camouflage that they almost literally disappeared into the surrounding trees.

Jack scanned the area though his field glasses, noting the slave corral, the temple steps, the lagoon, and the relative distances between each landmark. *Hold on—the lagoon!* His binoculars panned back along the still water of the lake, and there she was: colossal, black, and torpedo-shaped, bearing the Silver

Star insignia.

"Whoa there!" Jack exclaimed in a harsh whisper.

Deadeye squinted out through a grid of strangler fig branches. "Well I'll be..."

Doc took the glasses from Jack and looked toward the lagoon. "The *Luftpanzer*," she hissed.

"No wonder the radio detector didn't pick her up," Duke muttered. "She's below the trees, totally masked by the jungle."

"There's the Temple of the Elders that Alanna mentioned," Doc said, pointing at the pyramid of stone steps across the camp.

Jack nodded. "And the whole place is crawling with Silver Star commandos. Deadeye, what do you make of it?"

Charlie leaned forward, peering out from the hollow. "I count at least three dozen Silver Star," he said. "Looks like four, maybe six officers and ten civilian workers, plus native labor."

"They couldn't have all come on that zeppelin," Doc protested.

Jack pointed at the handmade pier in the distance. "Some seaplanes moored on the lake," he said. "And three... no, four troop trucks at the south end."

"Which means there must be a navigable road out of the jungle," said Duke.

Doc nodded. "And begs the question where they're getting land-based assistance."

"How much heavy armament?" Duke asked.

Jack squinted through the binoculars. "I can see two heavy machine guns," he said. "And they're both trained on that corral full of prisoners."

As Jack estimated the dimensions of the slave pen, Deadeye suddenly perked up.

"I can see Rivets," he announced. "Looks like he's okay."

Doc fell into her overcautious battlefield nurse persona. "We must assume sidearms and rifles on each of the commandos."

Deadeye almost chuckled. "Yeah, but those Mauser rifles are heavy and won't be much use in close quarters."

"Hey," Jack said, flashing a smile at Doc. "It's only three-to-one odds. We can take 'em."

"Three-to-one is still in their favor," Doc chided. "No reason not to be prepared."

"Fair enough," Jack said. His binoculars scanned up the stone stairway to the apex of the ancient pyramid. "We need a diversion to draw attention away from the heavy guns so we can free the prisoners and keep Crowley from completing whatever ritual he has up his sleeve."

Doc scowled. "And with this many potential

sacrifices, it must be something big. A summoning of some kind…"

Suddenly Katoc leaped from his perch to
meet the trio of scouts he'd sent on the north-
ern trail. They exchanged a few words in a di-
alect of Kayapô, and Katoc turned to Jack.

"Jack Mah-grah," he said urgently. "Silver
Star patrol not far. Three men. Not far."

Jack brightened. "Charlie, come with me,"
he ordered. "Doc, you and Duke stay here
with the munitions. I have an idea."

- Chapter 17 -

Katoc led Jack and Deadeye back to the fork in the trail, and the trio headed north along what appeared to be a deer path along the western shore of the lake. After another half mile, the trail intersected with a footpath from the south. They found some high ground in the form of an ancient stone outcropping which towered a dozen feet over the trail. Without a word, Deadeye found cover across the trail at the base of a hollowed-out mahogany tree. Katoc merged with the green veil of ivy and strangler fig vines behind the rock, nocking a long hunting arrow into his bow. Jack looked back at him and pointed at the side of his throat to indicate the desired target. Katoc nodded.

Three commandos in gray cotton fatigues and black military caps tromped down the trail, Mauser rifles slung over sweaty shoulders. Jack reached instinctively for one of his pistols, but remembered stealth was the name of the game, and he slid it back into his holster. But in doing so, he made the slightest of scratching noises as the shifting leather holster slid across the stone overhang.

That was all the Silver Star lieutenant needed to hear. He raised his hand in caution, and the other two men stopped, unshouldering their rifles. The lieutenant drew a Luger from his belt holster and stepped forward slowly, eyes scanning the green curtain of jungle.

Jack realized they'd already lost the element of absolute surprise, and with each passing moment the risk of being discovered increased exponentially. He flagged Katoc and leaped from the rock onto the second man. The lieutenant spun around to see Jack land on his comrade. He aimed his Luger with the intent to fire it, but his neck and throat exploded in pain, and he watched the arrow point thrust out from the indentation above his Adam's apple. He staggered momentarily, gushing blood from his throat.

The third commando ratcheted the bolt back on his Mauser rifle, but didn't have time to aim before Deadeye spun from behind the mahogany tree and opened the man's throat with his trench knife.

Jack leveled a wallop to the second commando's jaw, sending him sprawling to the dirt, unconscious. He turned toward the lieutenant, who remained standing, looking awkwardly at the arrow shaft protruding from his neck. Jack cocked back a fist and knocked his lights out. The lieutenant fell, and almost immediately the three bodies began to smolder and smoke.

Katoc watched the spectacle from atop the overhang, unwilling to come into closer contact with such magic. Jack and Deadeye wasted no time in stripping their uniforms and weapons, leaving nothing but three piles of rapidly decaying bones which they kicked into the gullies on either side of the trail. Jack didn't like the idea of not giving human remains a proper burial, especially given the chances of them coming back strapped to a rocket. But he knew these men had made their choices, and a proper burial was never part of the plan. The Silver Star were all about the essence of life, and each and every one of them had pledged theirs to Crowley.

The uniforms themselves were unharmed, although two of them were stained with a fair amount of blood.

They folded the uniforms, shouldered the weapons, and headed back to the camp overlook at a quick run. As they approached the tangled mess of tropical trees and vines, they were met by Duke's service revolver.

"Who goes there?" he demanded.

Jack walked out of the foliage carrying the new uniforms. "The one and only Captain Stratosphere," he quipped.

Doc was on her feet immediately. "What are you holding—? Are those Silver Star uniforms?"

Deadeye smiled. "That's right."

Jack tossed the uniforms on the ground and winked at Doc as he unshouldered one of the Mauser rifles. "Doc," he said, "I'm afraid I'm going to have to take you prisoner."

# # #

Jack didn't like the stiff collar of the Silver Star uniform. Although made for tropical climes, it was still heavy, itchy, and far too hot. The lieutenant's uniform was also black, as opposed to the charcoal gray of the lower ranks, and Jack shook his head as he tried to figure out what they were thinking, sending black uniforms into hot environments such as this.

Perhaps, thought Jack, *it's a form of torment for Crowley's pleasure.*

Once Jack, Duke, and Deadeye had squirmed into captured uniforms and crammed feet into boots a size too small, Katoc sent the other hunters scattering into the jungle around the camp to await the signal. And Jack had made sure it would be unmistakable.

Jack bound Doc at the wrists with tent

cord in a knot she could easily escape, and the three "Silver Star commandos" marched their captive toward the camp. Deadeye was worried at first that he might not pass among the Silver Star's Aryan majority, however Doc assured him their membership included acolytes and soldiers from all peoples of the world, and she'd seen a couple Hindustani soldiers at this very camp. Though not East Indian, Deadeye wouldn't arouse suspicion unless he drew unnecessary attention to himself. He was used to playing it cool.

Jack took point, dressed as the late lieutenant. Doc followed, flanked by Duke and Deadeye, rifles at the ready. To their absolute surprise, nobody took notice of them. Business continued in all corners of the camp, with captives hauling debris and soldiers supervising work details. Jack began hearing a faint voice of doubt in the back of his mind, telling him this had been too easy. They'd gotten within a few yards of the prisoner corral when a tall, uniformed figure stepped into their path, blocking the way.

"Who is this?" Captain Ecke demanded. His blue eyes pierced the dappled haze of the campground, his grizzled face a throwback to an earlier era of bearded sea captains, shipwrecks, and tall tales.

Jack stopped in his tracks, thinking quickly. Ecke spoke in English, which meant he was used to dealing with a multicultural force. Still, he felt he'd trigger fewer alarms if he at least feigned a modicum of Germanic background. "Dorothy Starr, *mein Kapitän*," he said in slightly German-accented English. "Medical officer on the *Daedalus*."

Ecke looked Doc over, noted her bonds were secure, and turned his attention back to the blond junior officer before him. "I don't recognize you, Lieutenant," he said, looking sidelong at Jack. "You are not assigned to the *Luftpanzer*?"

"*Nein*," Jack replied, hoping it wasn't too overdone. "I was in the advance guard, with Herr Crowley."

The airship captain regarded them for another moment.

"Very well," he said finally. "Take her to the pen with the others. I presume Crowley's madness will get underway momentarily."

"*Jawohl, mein Kapitän*," Jack saluted, clicking his boot heels together like he'd seen German officers do in the war. To his delight, Ecke returned the salute and stalked off toward the motor pool. Either Silver Star protocol was steeped in German military tradition, or their ranks were filled with veterans who maintained them out of habit.

As they watched him leave, Doc whispered, "Jack, that was Captain Jonas Ecke of the

Luftpanzer. He was a zeppelin captain during the war."

"He destroyed a quarter of London," Duke muttered, "and they say he never lost a ship."

Jack stared after him. "Let's make sure that record gets challenged before we're through here," he said, nodding to Duke. "You know what to do."

"One rather large diversion, coming up," said Duke.

"Okay, Charlie," Jack said. "Let's get Doc into the pen."

Doc scowled. "I won't forget this, Jack."

"I don't suppose you will."

They began to close the remaining distance to the corral, and Duke silently pulled away from the group, trudging off toward the trail head.

There was a single guard posted at the corral gate, and he saluted Jack as he approached with Doc, with Deadeye bringing up the rear.

"Another sacrifice for our master," Jack informed the guard.

"*Sehr gut!*" the man replied, unlatching the rattan gate and opening it for his superior officer.

Jack stood to the side as Deadeye guided Doc into the corral, which was filled with exhausted natives and one very demoralized mechanic. Jack leaned in as she passed, whispering in her ear.

"See to Rivets and follow our lead."

Doc nodded. The gate was barred behind her, and Jack strolled across the last quarter of the camp, toward what looked like an access road through the jungle. Deadeye wandered over behind one of the two machine gun emplacements and leaned on the heavy Mauser rifle.

Doc angled her way through the crowd of natives to where Rivets leaned against the rattan corral walls. She immediately pulled her hands free of the ropes which had bound her, and slipped a camp knife out of her left boot.

"Boy, am I glad to see you," Rivets muttered as Doc cut his hands free.

"Are you hurt?" Doc asked.

"Just my pride," Rivets answered. "What's the plan?"

"Keep your eyes open and follow Jack's lead."

Rivets grunted a half smile. "Oh, so the usual plan."

Doc worked through the crowd, cleaving their bonds.

The low crash of a metal gong echoed through the camp.

Jack looked toward the sky above the lake clearing. The sun had dipped below the treetops, coloring everything in bold hues of purple and orange. He took up a nonchalant posture near the motor pool, watching as a procession of Silver Star acolytes filtered out of the camp tents and traversed the clearing. Each wore mystics' robes, the result of a European fetish for Egyptian occultism, complete with an iridescent blue *uraeus* headdress. Arms bared, they marched single file toward the temple pyramid, carrying lit candles before them. At the temple base, they broke into two equal lines, climbing either side of the main stairway toward the altar before they stopped and faced inward across from each other.

A figure clad in the robes of a high priest appeared at the summit of the stairway, arms raised. *It must be Crowley,* Jack realized. His hunch was confirmed when Silver Star troops began to point up at the altar, exclaiming things like, "Look there! Atop the temple! Our master speaks!"

Crowley's voice was higher-pitched than Jack had imagined, but it carried through the natural resonating chamber of the jungle clearing. "*Behold this bleeding breast of mine —gashed with the sacramental sign!*" he blared, drawing a large ceremonial knife across the bulk of his chest. The wound became a red stripe, seeping blood.

Jack stared, awestruck at the ritual taking place at the altar above. He became suddenly aware of the bulk of his .45s, pinching his calves from within his Silver Star boots. He was itching for a fight he knew to be inevitable.

Crowley lifted what appeared to be a round hardtack biscuit from the altar above his head, then wet it in the blood oozing from the wound on his chest. An ominous crack of thunder came from nowhere, sending a chill through all present.

"I stanch the Blood; the wafer soaks
It up, and the high priest invokes!"

He broke off a small bit of the hardtack and ate it. Jack shuddered.

"This Bread I eat. This Oath I swear
As I enflame myself with prayer:
'There is no grace: there is no guilt:
This is the law; DO WHAT THOU WILT!'"

Another clap of thunder echoed through the jungle.

Ready, Charlie, Jack thought. *Come on, Duke...*

Then Crowley stepped in front of the altar and glared down over his followers, still brandishing the long knife in a bloody hand. "Bring forth the sacrifices!"

Jack cast a worried glance at the slave pen and saw a tall, slender woman in a black officer's uniform gesture with the familiar bejeweled Cross of Cadiz, pointing one of the prisoners out to the guard.

No surprise this is where that thing ended up, Jack thought.

The woman stood by the gate as the soldier entered and pushed his way through the natives, returning with Doc at gunpoint. The tall woman drew her own Luger pistol and directed Doc toward the pyramid, and the soldier locked the corral again.

He didn't recognize the rank of her insignia, but Jack realized the woman must be of some importance in the Silver Star organization, possibly subordinate only to Crowley himself, judging by the deference shown her by the other soldiers. Jack cautiously knelt down as if adjusting an uncomfortable boot, watching as Doc was pushed up to the stone stairway that led to a bloody death.

Doc scanned the crowd for Jack, and they locked eyes briefly. The nod he gave was all but imperceptible, but it meant the world to her.

Then Maria's gun was pressing into her back and they began climbing the steps. Another crack of thunder, and Doc could see the red shimmer of the world being warped behind the altar.

- Chapter 18 -

Duke got to the trail head and disappeared along the deer path heading north along the lake, shedding the Silver Star uniform jacket and cap as he went. Katoc was waiting for him at the edge of the forest on the north shore of the lake, the canvas satchel from the *Daedalus* slung across his body. A group of four Tree People warriors stood by in the darkening jungle.

Without exchanging a word, Katoc handed the satchel to Duke, who waved them all to follow him. Then he was off the trail and scurrying overland, cutting across the lake shore under the shadow of the trees. Before long, they stood alongside the impressive silhouette of the *Luftpanzer*, colossal and black and bristling with weapons. It was moored at the surface of the lake, anchored at the nose and tail, plus an additional anchor from each side. The electric lights in the gondola were on, but Duke could sense no movement within.

He pantomimed swimming to Katoc, who nodded enthusiastically. Fortunately, Duke didn't need to worry about his munitions get-

208

ting wet, as they functioned on friction and not black powder. He slung the satchel around on his back with the strap cutting across his neck, and quietly waded into the water, followed by Katoc and his warriors.

The half-dozen raiders pushed silently through the silky lake, now black with orange highlights from the sunset. A few paces in, the soft sand floor dropped away and they were swimming. Thirty yards through the dark water and they found themselves at the *Luftpanzer*'s gondola. Dim amber light shone out through the windows, creating small fractals of gold on the shimmering lake surface.

Katoc and two of the warriors swam to the anchor line at the nose and began to shimmy up, toward the bridge. Duke found himself amidships with the two remaining warriors, both female, from Queen Alanna's royal guard. They made their way under the gondola to one of the boarding hatches, and Duke grasped the locking handle. He gestured for the two royal guards to quickly enter the ship, and that is exactly what they did.

Duke propped the hatch open and the royal guards were already inside, rolling to the floor and coming up with weapons ready. A solitary Silver Star airship trooper who'd been snoozing in the main saloon woke and turned on the boarding party with Luger drawn. He was neutralized instantly by one of the guard women, his throat opened with her antler knife. He immediately began to sizzle and decay. Duke pulled himself into the gondola, struggling with the weight of the now-soaked canvas satchel.

The royal guards took up defensive positions by the hatches at either end of the main saloon, and Duke found himself reverse-engineering the giant airship in his mind. He'd never been on an aircraft this massive, but he reckoned the gas cells were pretty much in the same place as any other dirigible. They had to find a ladder up.

The tropical heat necessitated keeping any windows which could to remain open, much to the bridge crew's ultimate chagrin. Katoc and his two braves found open window panels on the bridge and were on the skeleton crew with bone knives and fists in an instant. The only trooper to put up a fight, the backup navigator, produced a stiletto from his belt and made short work of the smaller native warrior, savagely opening the crook of his neck just above collarbone. Katoc responded with his own obsidian blade, driving it through the base of the navigator's skull. There was no other resistance, and the episode had remained relatively silent, save for the chants wafting in from the temple across the lake. Katoc and his associate watched in horror as the Silver Star troops melted and dissolved into ash and bone fragments, then they headed aft.

Duke climbed the perforated aluminum ladder two steps at a time. Soaking wet from the lake and his own sweat, he felt a draft move up his back and he shivered. There before him was the main gantry through the center of the ship. It ran from the metal landing grate to the stern, over six hundred feet, and into a hazy obscurity. On either side, in reinforced vulcanized canvas ballonets, was enough hydrogen to burn down a small city.

A Silver Star airman came stalking out of the dark, knife drawn, as firearms were forbidden in the area. Then a native javelin pierced his chest, and he stumbled and sprawled on the deck. Duke turned to see both royal guard women ascending the landing. He thanked them, but beckoned them to head back down to the gondola—and if it looked like the ship was on fire, to get the hell off.

Squinting into the dark, Duke took the wet satchel from his shoulder. He dug out one the heavy spheres from the bag and surged forward by sheer will, regardless of any hidden danger. Were there any more airmen with knives lurking down the hallway? He sure didn't know, and anyone waiting down the gantry was about to be shown the inherent dangers of hydrogen lift gas. At Ballonnet 3, Duke thumbed the trigger that popped open the metallic globe of the Tesla Grenade, flipped the toggle that engaged the battery, and dropped it back into the satchel with its brothers and sisters.

Then he shoved the satchel into the crevice between Ballonets 3 and 5, opened a twelve-inch seam in Ballonet 3 with his trench knife, and ran like hell.

# # #

The air behind Crowley grew blurry and swelled as if ready to give birth. Electric tendrils erupted from the eye of the phenomenon, crawling over the altar and across the stone floor. The mage continued his chant, calling forth the demon Choronzon. The initial appearance was relatively easy, but creating a large enough power pool to actually open a portal to bring the entity through—much less bind it to one's will—would take all the blood in the slave pen.

Crowley continued his invocation:

"I entered with woe; with mirth
I now go forth, and with thanksgiving,
To do my pleasure on the earth
Among the legions of the living...
Nuit, Hadit, Ra-Hoor-Khuit..."

The crowd of soldiers and acolytes answered the phrase in kind.

"Nuit, Hadit, Ra-Hoor-Khuit..."

Doc and Maria were perhaps a dozen steps up the pyramid when the lake and surrounding jungle lit up like a bonfire. Maria stopped, aghast at the sight of the *Luftpanzer* bursting into fire in sections.

Doc knew what was coming, and she took the opportunity to duck and twist backward, thrusting her elbow into Maria's ribs, sending her backward into one of the candle-holding acolytes, which set his gauzy robes afire and sent her Luger skittering off the pyramid steps.

Chaos erupted with the hydrogen from the zeppelin's gas cells.

Deadeye leaped into the circle of sandbags around the first machine gun emplacement, clubbing both Silver Star commandos in the skull with the butt of his Mauser rifle. He dropped the rifle and angled the surplus Lewis gun at the lone slave pen guard. The machine gun chattered and the guard was ripped apart. Then he sprinted to the corral and flung the gate open, letting the native hostages run free. Most ran to the cover of the trees. Some who still had a bit of strength attacked the closest troops and took their guns.

Rivets ran to the first Lewis gun and started picking off troops as they scurried to the motor pool. One truck pulled away into the jungle and a second exploded in flames, peppered with rounds from Rivets' machine gun.

All eyes on the pyramid turned to the exploding airship on the lake, and Doc took advantage of the moment to leap down the stairs, beyond the reach of Maria Blutig, who had just separated herself from the burning acolyte. Maria caught the motion and turned to follow, knocking over two more robed cultists.

The jungle came alive with poisoned darts and long hunting arrows, skewering panicked soldiers. Some troops returned fire, shooting blindly into the jungle. Jack and Deadeye immediately shed their Silver Star uniform jackets, a signal to the native hunters not to target them.

Deadeye ran to the second machine gun and pummeled both soldiers unconscious. Then he panned the Lewis gun around on its tripod to face the camp.

The *Luftpanzer* continued to burst into flames, front to back, one section at a time. Captain Ecke stood helplessly on the small pier extending from the south shore, watching her die in pieces. He became suddenly aware of the chaos in the camp, and took off running toward the pyramid—and the troop truck he knew was parked behind it.

Atop the pyramid, Crowley was a seething ball of rage.

"Infidels!" he shrieked from the altar. "Deceivers!"

Two elite Silver Star agents pounced immediately, pulling him away from the altar and ushering him down the back stairway.

A demonic claw penetrated the shimmering membrane behind the altar, catching one of the elder acolytes by his robes. The elder screamed and his body popped and contorted as the demon pulled it through the tiny hole between dimensions. The elder's blood seemed to bolster the incomplete spell—to strengthen Choronzon—and the membrane became thinner.

Maria leaped over burning cultists to close the distance with Doc.

Doc was well ahead, but missed her footing on the final step. She felt her left ankle give way and she sprawled on the jungle floor. A strong hand pulled her upright, and she found herself face to face with Jack McGraw.

"You okay?" he asked.

Doc winced and grunted, "Ankle." She looked up at the roiling, expanding rift above the pyramid, and her jaw went slack. "Oh no..."

Jack wrapped his left arm around her waist, pointing the .45 in his right hand at Maria. "Stop right there!" he ordered, then he blinked and looked again. It couldn't be her.

Maria froze, shock and realization on her face. "You!" she gasped. "Jack McGraw!"

Jack gaped at her. "Maria Gunnhild?"

"Blutig," Maria corrected.

"Bloody Mary?" Jack smirked. "Are you serious?"

Doc frowned. "You know this woman?"

"She worked at a bar in Beauvois during the war, under a fake name," he explained. "But her real job was as a spy for the Central Powers. The Allies used her to spread false intelligence back to the enemy."

Maria's face swelled red with fury at this revelation, but she had one of her own. "You shot down Hans Heinrich!"

Jack glared back at her, wondering at the significance.

"You killed my betrothed—you killed my heart!"

It suddenly sank in—this woman had been driven mad with grief and anger, her quest for vengeance fueled by Crowley's megalomania and resources. And now she had occult knowledge and a paramilitary army at her disposal.

Doc lunged for the Cross of Cadiz in Maria's hand, wrenching it out of her grip. But the surge of proximity energy from the lodestone in her pocket burned and numbed her entire leg, and she crumpled on her bad ankle, pulling Jack off balance. She dropped the cross and winced in agony.

Maria angled up the stairs and leaped off the far side of the stairway, disappearing toward the lake shore.

Jack glanced around. Troop trucks were already making for the jungle trail. The pyramid stairway was a trail of burning cultists and dead commandos. At the top, an ancient demon threatened to burst into their world.

Deadeye and Rivets ran to the bottom of the pyramid, where Jack was trying to hold Doc upright.

"J-Jack," she stammered.

"Where's Crowley?" Deadeye asked.

Jack nodded toward the trail. "Flew the coop," he said. "Maria's heading for one of those planes. Get Doc back to the tree city. I'm going after this one!"

Before Doc could argue, he'd all but flung her onto his two comrades, then he was gone.

Doc reached for him in vain. "Jack, no!"

Rivets shook his head. "Let's go, Doc," he said. "No use tryin' to talk him out of it."

Doc pulled back. "You don't understand," she urged. "The spell Crowley started is still going, and it's taken on a life of its own. If we don't close the rift and banish that demon, it'll get through!"

"Get through?" Rivets asked, completely dumbfounded.

Deadeye looked Doc over, not wild about

her condition. "You sure you're up for that?" he asked. "I mean, do you know how?"

Doc stared at the crackling portal above and shook her head.

"I don't know," she shrugged. "But I have to try."

- Chapter 19 -

Doc limped up the pyramid stairs, Rivets on her left, Deadeye on her right. She gripped the Cross of Cadiz in her right hand, leaning on her two crewmates and wincing with every step. Her left ankle was a swollen beehive of pain, and her right thigh felt as if the lodestone had burned a hole in it. About halfway up, a robed acolyte leaped out of the night on the stairs above them, and Deadeye snapped off a shot from his temporary Luger. The cultist spun away and flopped down the stairs like a discarded rag doll.

The membrane between the world and whatever putrid dimension Chroronzon called home shimmered and warped, revealing the entity's entire reddish-black, scaly arm. It extended a good dozen feet beyond the portal and continued to slash with savage claws. The impossibly low rumble of its demonic choir vibrated through the ancient stone stairs, and the trio stumbled with every third or fourth step.

Doc could hardly stand, let alone walk. Rivets and Deadeye all but carried her.

As they neared the apex, they could see the sundered bones of the elder priest scattered across the stairs, streaked with blood.

The transparent membrane between the dimensions pulsed and stretched, and Doc saw the creature's yellow eye peering at her from beyond the rift. The demon's beastly arm grabbed and swiped at them, as fingers of lightning traced the altar. A sound like metal straining under high tension groaned from the weakening portal.

Doc pulled her right arm from behind Deadeye and held the Cross of Cadiz in front of her. Reaching toward the portal, she closed her eyes and began to move her hand in a counter-clockwise motion, her fingers gripping the artifact just below the horizontal arms of the crosspiece. She could feel the pulse of energy radiate from its core, and heard its high-pitched tone begin to emanate from all around. Her ankle throbbed spikes of agony with every heartbeat. She tried to recall her occult studies—any arcane portal-closing spell would do—but nothing came. She decided to abandon dogma and trust her instinct and sheer will. And perhaps the innate properties of the holy artifact in her hand.

Then she closed her eyes and thrust the cross forward. It glowed with impossible intensity, as if she held a star, ringing with a high, pulsing celestial tone. The magic-detecting stone in her pocket burned and seared her thigh. She cried out in pain, almost dropping where she stood, but Rivets and Deadeye held her fast.

Her arm continued its counter-clockwise circles, and she heard Oba speak as if from within the stone itself.

"Papa Legba, Guardian of the Crossroads, let this nexus be closed!"

She remembered, as she'd held the dying *bokor* in the old Spanish fort, how he'd grasped the lodestone with the last of his strength. He must have infused his own soul into it.

He's here, she thought. *Right here in the stone!*

Reaching across her body with her left hand, she dug the lodestone from her pocket and held it parallel with the Cross of Cadiz. She felt a surge of power from deep within her aching body travel up through her arm, and through the conduit of the lodestone filled with Oba's spirit. The high-tension groan became a storm of conflicting sound. Lightning shot in desperate tendrils across the pyramid. One caught Rivets square in the chest, throwing him back down several steps, unconscious. Another threw Deadeye clear off the main stairs onto the side. A third hit Doc's injured foot, traveled up her leg and through her chest, filling her with a pain she'd never known. She collapsed like a lump of clay where she'd stood, her heartbeat shallow and random. Every nerve was fire.

Doc weakly opened her eyes and watched the portal contract and seal itself with an explosion of wind and light.

An unholy shriek echoed through the jungle as Choronzon's severed arm dropped to the altar. Its clawed hand gripped the edge of the stone table, then lay still.

The Cross of Cadiz blinked once more and extinguished its light. The lodestone went dark, immediately cool against Doc's hand.

Delirious with pain, she muttered, "Jack..." and passed out.

# # #

Jack leaped down the side stairs of the Temple of the Elders, trying to close the gap with Maria. He couldn't believe the person who had been dogging their trail all this time was the fiancé of the German ace he'd shot down while saving Stede Bonnet over France. *No matter,* he thought. *I'll finish this tonight. One way or another.*

As his boots hit ground at the foot of the pyramid, he could barely make out Maria's running form along the pier in the distance, silhouetted by the burning canvas of the *Luft-*

panzer. Its aluminum frame was bent and broken, looking like the ribcage of a colossal beast as it sank into the lake.

Jack found his footing on the long wooden pier. Already he could hear one of the Caspar engines rev. She was trying to fly out of here.

He wasn't going to let that happen without a challenge.

Jogging down the narrow dock with only the moon and the dying fire of the giant airship to light his way, Jack finally arrived at one of three Caspar U.1 seaplanes moored with their noses facing in. Its cantilevered wings had no struts or wires between them. He could make out the shape of a Lewis gun mounted to the upper wing. At least there was armament.

There was a mooring line for each float, and he cast them both off, giving the plane a push backward as he climbed aboard.

The cockpit was small and the controls a no-frills affair. The Caspar U.1 was designed to be light and small, and to fit within a transport cylinder for submarine launch. What it lacked in strength, speed, and comfort, it made up for in ease of setup. Jack hit the ignition and the 5-cylinder radial engine sputtered to life. He revved it hard and used his feet to rudder the plane in a short turn. He felt down in the cubby by the seat and found a pair of cheap pilot goggles.

Better than nothing, he thought, and snapped them over his head.

Maria's plane was already in the air, illuminated by the rising moon.

Jack throttled forward, maximum speed. The lake became black silk under him, the sinking *Luftpanzer* a deadly beacon to his right. He pulled back on the stick, and the Caspar nosed into the air, trailing water from the airborne floats.

The moon shone bright over the jungle, casting a blue-white blanket over the dark green canopy. Jack climbed in a slow corkscrew, keeping an eye on the plane in the distance. When he finally found the right altitude and air current to compliment his speed and angle of attack, he throttled forward, pushing the little plane to its top speed of 90 miles per hour.

The jungle trees whisked by underneath. In the distance ahead, he could see Maria banking into a turn. Clearly she knew that Jack was as tenacious an enemy as she.

Jack McGraw had flown nighttime raids and covert missions during the war, but never had the personal stakes been higher. He stood up in the pilot's seat and tilted the Lewis gun back to check the disc-shaped magazine on the top of the weapon. It was full. He pulled back hard on the cocking bolt, readying the gun for use, then sat back in his seat. He didn't fasten the belt, as he knew mobility might be at a premium, and if he had to invert, he felt that he could brace with his legs to keep from falling.

Maria's plane completed its turn and was now facing Jack's. For an uncomfortable minute, the two planes barreled toward each other, the only sound the roar of the rotary engines. Then, when Jack had approximated the range of the Lewis, he reached for the trigger. There was a loud clack and the gun was silent. It had jammed.

Maria's plane screamed toward Jack, her Lewis gun barking. Jack instinctively banked his plane away from the onslaught, taking a few rounds of incoming fire on the floats and belly of the Caspar. Every fourth round was a green-white blaze of light. Then they were past each other, banking around for another pass. But Jack knew he couldn't clear his jammed machine gun while setting up another pass.

This was like a medieval joust, except Jack had no lance.

Maria banked in a hard turn. She'd seen his plane take damage and was emboldened by that.

Jack was out of options. He throttled forward and hauled back on the stick, climbing into the night sky.

He rolled out of the climb and felt his stomach leap in the moment without gravity, then his legs clamped to the outer edges of the cockpit to keep him in place, and he pitched forward into a sharp dive.

Maria lined up her shot and relaxed the throttle, letting him come to her. The Lewis gun chattered away, sending bright tracers into the night sky.

Jack felt the impact of bullets on the nose of the plane, sparks erupting from the engine cowling and propeller. They were just a few yards away now, Jack's engine puffing with flame and spraying oil.

Twenty yards. Ten.

Maria's gun tore into the fuselage of Jack's plane, and his left leg erupted in pain as a tracer bullet found its way into his thigh.

Suddenly Jack banked over hard, belly toward Maria's aircraft. They collided almost head-on with Jack's plane at a 90-degree aspect. His floats sandwiched both of Maria's left wings, and the force of his diving plane sheared them clean away. He throttled back and banked out of his dive, turning to see Maria's plane spinning to a fiery crash in the trees below.

Jack didn't have any time to celebrate. His engine sputtered flames—which were quickly spreading to the cockpit—and the fuselage looked like a cheese grater. The left float snapped and came away, falling to the jungle like a brick. The plane was going down. Whether it burned before or after the impending crash was a moot point. He wiped engine oil from his goggles and did some quick math.

He could try to land the plane in the tree canopy and likely burn in the process, or he could trust his luck and leap, hoping for some sort of purchase in the foliage—and not the more likely impalement on a random tree branch, being crushed by his own flaming airplane, or bleeding out from the bullet wound in his thigh.

Searing fire whipped at his face and his instinct took over.

He stood in the pilot seat and jumped into the moonlit sky.

His flailing hand caught hold of something and it startled him. Looking up, he saw he'd grasped the metal rung of a chain ladder. He followed the ladder upward to see it terminate at the giant, round silhouette of a hot air balloon. Then he realized the engine he was hearing wasn't his own plane, which became a fiery mass in the trees below.

"Hang on, my friend!" called a booming voice from above.

Jack couldn't believe it. "Stede??" he cried.

The voice above laughed, and Jack could feel himself being hauled aloft with the ladder.

Then there were two pairs of hands on him, hauling him over the side into the open gondola.

"Stede Bonnet..." Jack muttered tiredly, dizzy from shock and loss of blood. "Thank you."

The Caribbean sky pirate knelt down to survey the damage. Jack would live, though he'd be limping awhile.

"I told you Bonnet's Brigands would be there in your time of need," Stede grinned.

- Chapter 20 -

By the time Katoc's warriors had returned to the Tree City—with Doc in a makeshift sling across the back of a brawny hunter—Jack was already being seen to by the village healers in the great hall. Stede's balloon *Revenge* floated tethered to one of many wooden guardrails that lined the pathways of the city, and native warriors dropped caches of Silver Star weapons and supplies at Queen Alanna's feet.

The people of the canopy had done well. They'd rescued their hostages, driven the evil Sky People out of the Temple of the Elders, and had become wealthy in trade goods. They'd only lost four of their number: one young brave at the *Luftpanzer*, and three hostages who had been gunned down while fleeing back to the jungle. They celebrated in groups around fire braziers strewn about the city, drumming, singing, and dancing well into the night.

Duke found Stede outside the great hall, sipping from a bottle of Bahamian rum.

"Captain Bonnet," Duke greeted. "How

good of you to make our little soiree."

Stede handed the bottle to Duke and grinned, and his white teeth were in such contrast to his skin that for a moment—at least against the backdrop of night—he almost appeared as Lewis Carroll's Cheshire Cat. "I see you made a nice bonfire out of that zeppelin," he winked.

"We did indeed," Duke nodded, taking a healthy swig from the bottle and handing it back. The burn in his throat was sorely welcomed. "I say, where's the rest of my crew?" he asked.

"They're in the great hall," Stede said. "All four of them were brought in wounded. The healers are tending them."

"Cheers, mate," Duke patted the larger man on the shoulder and ducked into the great hall to check on his friends.

Jack was high on some native draught derived from ground coca leaves, grinning like a fool as a native woman stitched up his leg. The bullet from Maria's Lewis gun sat in a bloody wooden bowl nearby.

Doc was likewise drugged, and was regaling anyone who would listen with the story of her facing down a demon and closing a dimensional portal. The severed arm had been brought back and was on display at the center of the great hall.

Deadeye and Rivets were given a natural sedative and some ancient prayers, their cuts bandaged with a poultice of Spanish moss and rubber tree sap.

As the sun rose searing white above the jungle, Doc found Jack leaning against a railing next to the great hall. Not a word was exchanged, nor were they necessary. She simply melted into his embrace and they stood like that for several minutes as the last of the cool night breezes escaped into the morning sky.

Alanna approached the two of them, her discerning look conspicuously absent. Her tone was soft and gregarious.

"My thanks, Jack Mah-grah," she said. "You have saved my people."

Jack gave a small bow in response. "We couldn't have done it without your brave warriors, Queen Alanna."

Alanna embraced Jack and Doc in turn. "You are now counted among my brave warriors. My friends," she said. "My Sky People."

Duke appeared behind her, flanked by Rivets and Deadeye.

"How did you like my diversion, Captain?" he asked, pushing the brim of his officer's cap up on his forehead.

Rivets clapped him on the back. "Heck of a show, Duke!"

"Couldn't have done it better myself,"

Deadeye quipped.

Duke smiled. "And don't you forget it, dear boy."

Jack didn't know if it was the native wacky juice he'd been given the previous night, or if he genuinely felt this good. His leg would be sore for a few days, but they'd done a great job tending the wound. It didn't feel infected. Still, there was work yet to be done.

"Say, Rivets," Jack said, "How long to repair the *Daedalus*... if she can be, that is?"

Rivets scratched his head and puzzled for a moment. "About a week, if I can get some parts in from Manaus," he said, adding, "and no interference."

"Fair enough," Jack said, noticing Stede's approach from the point where the *Revenge* was tethered. "Well done, everyone. And once again, thanks to Captain Bonnet for saving me at the last possible moment."

Stede gave Jack an index finger salute. "I'd say we're even now, eh?"

Doc's brow furrowed and she looked up at Jack. "Crowley was escorted away from the temple. He must have gotten out on one of the trucks. What of Maria?"

"She crashed," Jack said with authority. "In flames."

Doc sighed. "Score one for the heroes."

Jack gazed over her head and out across

the vast Amazon jungle.

"Yes. The heroes."

He thought of Maria and how she must have felt at the loss of her beloved. It was a natural response, to want vengeance against someone who had killed the love of your life. He couldn't blame her for the path she'd taken. Had the situation been reversed... had the fortunes of war gone differently... sure, they were heroes. But perhaps only because they'd been on the winning side.

No, he thought. *That's not true. We stopped an evil organization from summoning a demon from another dimension. We saved innocent lives. That must be worth something.*

Jack left a small kiss on the top of Doc's head. She smiled and held him tightly.

# # #

Sunlight streamed down through the forest, almost solid bars of light in the haze and steam rising from the jungle floor. A trail of airplane parts led to a grove of colossal wimba trees, like crooked fingers pointing up from the soil.

About twenty feet up, lodged in the first spread of branches, lay the smoldering hulk of the Caspar, both of its left wings sheared off, the right wings bent upward. Smoke still wafted from the broken skeleton of the aircraft.

Both floats were strewn across the jungle in shattered pieces.

One half of the propeller was lodged in a tree sixty feet away.

The Lewis gun lay on its side, barrel twisted, at the side of a deer path not fifty yards north.

Along with a single set of bootprints, leading into the deep jungle.

- Chapter 21 -

Rivets got his truck full of parts from Manaus within a week, and, true to his word, the *Daedalus* was airborne five days later. Duke helped repair the ship where Rivets would let him, but the crew spent most of the intervening time learning the language and customs of the Tree People. Doc studied and polished the Cross of Cadiz, wrapping it in a yard of native cloth and securely housing it in a mahogany box—both items gifts from Queen Alanna.

Another trophy for the occult experts at AEGIS to put in their case. She was glad Crowley's minions had brought it to the Amazon, anyway. Hopefully they would never need it in the field again.

The Tree People sent daily scouting parties to the Temple of the Elders to take whatever was useful and hide the rest. At no point did the Silver Star return. Jack assumed Crowley would cut bait and run to set up his next operation. He was down a few dozen troops, a powerful artifact, a demon, and a very expensive airship. It would take time to lick his wounds and recoup his losses. And besides, it was his modus operandi.

When at last the *Daedalus* was sky-worthy, the crew exchanged farewells and small gifts with the Tree People of the Amazon, and were away.

Doc kept trying to get Jack alone to talk, but there never seemed to be a good time. They powered through four solid days of their northwesterly course, by way of Panama City, Managua and Acapulco, before arriving at Ryan Airport at Dutch Flats, San Diego, California. The airfield was small—literally a two-plane hangar with an adjacent office building near the Marine Corps Recruiting Depot—but AEGIS had a limousine waiting to take them into the city.

The limo dropped them in front of the US Grant Hotel on Broadway, and a small army of bellhops and attendants took their luggage inside. The heroes of the Amazon adventure—after action report case number SA05-25-2904-003—were given suites and room service. Legendary among politicians and the Hollywood elite, the Grant offered amenities like no other hotel. Jack wasn't sure he'd be able to sleep in such a comfortable bed, but he was sure going to try.

Edison had wired ahead, setting up a press conference to be followed by dinner with some Los Angeles film people the following day. After all, licensing the real-life adventures of the

Daedalus crew was a good way to bolster AEGIS funding while painting a complimentary picture of the organization. President Coolidge telephoned to congratulate the crew and invite them to the White House when they were back on the East Coast. When Rivets and Deadeye heard about their new schedule, they begged Jack in tandem if they could all go back to the Amazon. Doc assured them they didn't have to speak to the press if they didn't want to. They'd earned some time off.

And tonight was all theirs. Duke and Deadeye headed to the waterfront to see if they could find a speakeasy, while Rivets was content to hole up in his suite with unlimited room service and a bottle of Canadian hooch procured for him by the concierge, who apparently "knew a guy". Doc invited Jack to dinner, and he accepted with pleasure.

After a hot bath and a catch-up on some deferred grooming, Jack put on the freshly pressed clothes the hotel management had sent up: a light gray sport coat and pleated trousers, gray dress shoes and a fedora to match. He slapped his freshly-shaved cheeks with Williams Aqua Velva and exited his room, propping the gray hat on his slicked back hair. A few paces down the hall, he knocked on the door to Doc's suite. She opened it, looking lovely in a beige skirt and jacket with her long bob in curls.

"You clean up pretty good," Jack quipped.

"Not so bad yourself," Doc replied, smiling. "You ready?"

Jack offered an arm, and together the strode to the elevator, where a teenager in a dark green uniform and pillbox cap took them to the ground floor. They stepped out and found their way into the main lobby where an older gentleman in a tuxedo played Gershwin on a grand piano.

Jack rubbed his chin, trying to remember something. "Now, your aunts are Agnes and... Millicent?"

"Yes... Millie," Doc chuckled.

Jack nodded. "Millie. Got it."

"Don't be nervous," Doc said as she took his arm again and wandered toward the foyer.

"I'm not nervous," Jack said. "We're just meeting your aunts."

"Well, yes," Doc said, "and..."

Just then the doorman greeted a pair of middle-aged matrons in spring gowns and hats of taffeta. Between the two, clutching a hand apiece, was a young girl of six. She had radiant green eyes like Doc, but her strawberry blond hair and mischievous smile was more like...

"Mommy!" the girl cried, running to Doc, who squatted down and swept her into a hug.

"There's my girl!" Doc grinned.

Agnes and Millie were all hugs and kisses and smiles at seeing their only niece and what appeared to be a new beau. Introductions swirled like a Texas tornado, Doc's aunts sized up Jack in an instant, and finally Doc turned the little girl to face him.

Jack McGraw, ace pilot, adventurer, hero, took a knee and put out his hand. The girl shook it gingerly.

"Ellen," said Doc. "This is Captain Jack McGraw."

"Hello there, Ellen," Jack said.

"How do you do, Captain McGraw," Ellen greeted.

Jack smiled at her, and when she smiled back, it was just like looking in a mirror. The girl was the spitting image of him at that age.

Doc's eyes filled with tears.

Jack looked at Doc, startled. He silently mouthed, "*Me?*"

Doc gazed at him softly and nodded.

The End

ABOUT THE AUTHOR

Todd Downing's love affair with pulp adventure dates back to his consumption of classic radio dramas and comic books as a child in the 1970s, which broadened into a general appreciation for scifi and fantasy media of all kinds.

He grew up in the greater San Francisco Bay Area, writing and drawing from a young age, his works ever-present in school literary journals and newspapers, and eventually on film. He married his high school sweetheart and moved to Seattle in the early 1990s where he began to write professionally, and worked as an artist in the videogame industry until his publishing company became a full time operation.

As the co-founder and creative director of Deep7 Press, Downing was the primary author and designer of over fifty roleplaying titles, including *Arrowflight, RADZ, Airship Daedalus*, and the official *Red Dwarf* RPG. He continues to write genre fiction for stage, film, comics, audio, and adventure gaming products.

Widowed to cancer in 2005, Downing remarried in 2009 and currently enjoys an empty nest in Port Orchard, Washington, with his wife, two cats, an elderly German shepherd and a flock of unruly chickens.

Join the author's mailing list at:
www.todddowning.com

More *Airship Daedalus* & *AEGIS Tales* content:
www.airshipdaedalus.com

The adventures of the Airship Daedalus
continue in *Assassins of the Lost Kingdom*
by E.J. Blaine
AVAILABLE NOW!

Made in the USA
Columbia, SC
03 September 2017